ONCE UPON A TIDE

A MERMAID'S TALE

BY STEPHANIE KATE STROHM

DISNEY • HYPERION

LOS ANGELES   NEW YORK

First Edition, September 2021
1 3 5 7 9 10 8 6 4 2
FAC-020093-21211

Printed in the United States of America

This book is set in PT Serif/Paratype; Herschel Whole/Fontspring
Designed by Phil Buchanan

Library of Congress Control Number: 2020053189
ISBN 978-1-368-05443-0

Reinforced binding

Visit www.DisneyBooks.com

For my mom, and the first swim of every summer

CHAPTER ONE

There are a *lot* of misconceptions about being a princess.

But maybe the biggest misconception of all is that princesses don't kick tail.

This princess?

Yeah, she kicks tail.

"Last one to the anemone park is a blobfish!" I shout. Well, I don't *shout*—you can't really shout underwater. Merpeople communicate telepathically. We can hear each other's thoughts, but only the thoughts we *want* to be heard. And, honestly, thank Poseidon we don't hear every single thought. I can't imagine swimming through the sea, being bombarded by what every single merperson is wondering—what to have for dinner or what shells to wear tomorrow or whether the weather topside will affect the waves. But luckily, mer-telepathy is nothing like that. The way we "talk" is just like humans talking, only there isn't any sound. It's sort of like sending a message straight to someone's brain. Land-livers

don't get it at all, even though it's not that complicated—but that's a typical land-liver for you.

No imagination.

"Lana, you promised you wouldn't call me a blobfish anymore!" Aarav huffs. He's so far behind me I can barely hear his thoughts.

"Keep up, and I won't!"

I blast through a school of fusilier fish, their yellow tails swishing back and forth like crazy as their silver bellies glimmer in the clear water. As the fusiliers scatter, they reveal a coral outcrop. I swim over the coral, narrowly avoiding scraping my belly on the rough surface.

"Coral!" I call behind me. I may want to destroy Aarav, but I don't mean *literally*. He's the most forgetful, disorganized merperson I know—not to mention as slow as a manatee—but he's also the best little brother in all the seven seas.

I let out a few bubbles in a sigh while Aarav twists out of the way of the coral. It would be so typical of Aarav to collide with a coral outcropping even when he's had plenty of advance warning.

That's another land-liver thing—they think we're all graceful, floating around the ocean like little bubbles drifting peacefully through the waves. Clearly, those people have never seen Aarav. One time he swam headfirst into an abandoned lobster trap and got so tangled up, he was stuck there until a Sea Scout troop happened to pass by on a nature swim.

Safely past the coral, I propel myself through a tangle of kelp, twisting and turning to keep from getting stuck in the long green strands of seaweed stretching up toward the surface. With one last flick of my tail, I'm through, and then I can see it in the distance—the anemone park.

Clarion is the most beautiful kingdom under the sea, and the anemone park is my favorite place in all of Clarion. Anemones of all shapes, sizes, and colors line the ocean floor, thicker and more beautiful than any plush carpet or meadow of wildflowers you could see topside. Gently, I lower myself down on top of them, their squishy little tendrils comforting against my back. I blow a bubble and watch it float up, up, up to the surface.

Up to where Aarav will be tomorrow.

Without me.

Several minutes later, Aarav arrives, somersaulting toward the seafloor as he dramatically collapses, pretending to faint from exhaustion.

"Looks like slow and steady didn't win the race this time." I poke him, and he rolls over, laughing. *"Sailfish wins again!"*

"'The Blobfish and the Sailfish' is a fable, Lana, not a factual account of true events." He blows a bubble, and then I blow one, too, and we watch them float up, together. *"It's just supposed to teach perseverance. Literally, of course a sailfish is faster than a blobfish."*

"And a Lana is faster than an Aarav."

Aarav sighs. *"At least an Aarav is faster than a blobfish."*

"True!" That's Aarav, always looking for the positive. I blow a quick stream of bubbles toward the surface.

"Fourteen," Aarav counts as the last bubble disappears above us. *"Bet I know why that's on your mind. I can't believe it's finally here! Your birthday's tomorrow. It's a big deal."*

"I know." I'm practically glowing with pride. I look down at my hands, half expecting them to be see-through and luminous, like I'm part crystal jellyfish. *"Fourteen must seem like a big deal when you're a wee merbaby of twelve,"* I tease.

"I have the social and emotional maturity of a quinquagenarian," Aarav scoffs. *"Which is why I'm not going to deign to respond to your slanderous ageism. And also why I say fancy words like 'quinquagenarian' instead of simply merperson in their fifties."*

"My bad. Please forgive me. You're a very fancy prince with an excellent vocabulary."

"And you're a very speedy princess with a decent vocabulary. Who's going to be the best queen Clarion has ever had." Typical Aarav, to go from teasing to heartfelt in an instant. He's always ready to make any conversation into A Moment. Sometimes I think he might be part cephalopod, because he's got enough feelings for three hearts. *"I can't believe you're going to start learning how to run the kingdom. That's, like . . . very . . . serious."*

"I am very serious." I cross my eyes, stick out my tongue, and puff out my cheeks. Aarav laughs. But joking aside, I *am* serious about government. That's another misconception about princesses—people think we're just sitting around combing our hair with forks, waiting for a handsome prince to float by. As if. I want to learn how to be the best ruler I can.

One day, I'll be in charge of all of Clarion, just like my dad. And tomorrow, when I turn fourteen, I'll be taking government classes every day, learning about diplomacy, economics, foreign relations, statecraft, and, well, everything I'll need to become queen. I can't wait!

"*But I* seriously *can't believe you're not coming with me.*" Aarav sighs.

"*I know.*" I try to make my voice sound as sad as possible so Aarav doesn't think I'm excited about ditching him...but because I'm starting my lessons tomorrow, for the first time in seven years, I won't have to spend a week on land visiting our mother for the Royal Festival. I've got a get-out-of-the-festival-free pass, and I couldn't be happier about it.

"*You're gonna have more fun without me,*" I tell Aarav. He looks like he doesn't want to admit it, but deep down, we both know it's true. "*Come on. You* love *being on land. The horrible way it smells, the way it gets so hot and makes everyone all uncomfortable and sweaty, how itchy all the clothes are...*"

"*Lana!*" Aarav protests. "*Only you would think about those things. What about the warmth of the sun on your face?*"

"*Too hot,*" I complain.

"*The tingly sensation of air filling your lungs?*"

"*Too tingly.*"

"*Basketball?*"

"*Boring and the rules are too complicated.*"

"*Seeing Mom?*"

I pause. My other answers were mostly jokes, but seeing Mom is *actually* complicated—way more complicated than basketball. I don't understand how Aarav can be so happy to see her every year. She left us, after only a measly seven years under the water, because she missed sunshine and grass and clouds and all these stupid things she should have thought about *before* she married a merking and went through all the trouble of having the Royal Sorcerer of the Hills conjure up a magical tail and gills.

If she cared about us, she'd still be here. End of story. And nothing Aarav—or Mom—could possibly say will ever make me change my mind.

"*I bet this is going to be your best Royal Festival ever,*" I say eventually, and Aarav knows me well enough to understand that this means I don't want to talk about Mom. "*The hottest, and the itchiest, and the driest, and the smelliest . . . all the things you love about that miserable chunk of rock up there.*"

"*No matter how good the Royal Festival is, I'll still miss you,*" he says simply, and blows another bubble toward the surface.

I squeeze his hand. Even though I'm relieved I get to skip my forced annual visit topside, I'll miss him, too.

An enormous stream of bubbles blasts through the anemone park with enough force that it sends Aarav and me tumbling.

"*AAAAAA!*" I scream in a not-very-princess-like manner. In my head, I can hear Aarav shrieking like a dismayed dolphin. I flip, fins over face, until I finally land tail-up in a bed of slightly squashed purple anemones. I pat them gently, silently apologizing for the squashing. They may not be able to talk, but they're still alive after all.

When I finally get myself floating right side up, I'm sort of expecting to see a humpback whale behind that massive blast of bubbles, but no, it's my best friend, Prince Finnian of the

Warm Seas, holding a massive conch shell. Finnian may be much smaller than a humpback whale, but he could probably do a lot more damage.

"*What is* that?" I point at the conch, assuming it's the source of the bubble blast.

"*Isn't it awesome?*" Finnian gazes at the shell fondly. "*I found it in the armory.*"

"*You found it in the* armory?" I repeat with disbelief. "*You decided to unleash a* weapon *on your best friend?*"

"*And her unsuspecting little brother?*" Aarav grumbles.

"*It was clearly labeled 'nonlethal'!*" Finnian protests, innocent as an angelfish.

Ever since Finnian's mom, Queen Fetulah of the Warm Seas, arrived in Clarion on a diplomatic mission at the beginning of the summer, we've been hanging out all the time. Of course, Finnian and I have known each other since we were tiny merbabies disrupting royal functions by refusing to nap, but we've never gotten to spend so much time together before. This was supposed to be yet another in a long line of short political visits, but the Prime Minister of the Deepest Depths has been making waves about the new trade route Queen Fetulah wants to establish with Clarion. As the tricky treaty negotiations have stretched on, so has Finnian's stay.

And the best part? Finnian will be here for the whole school year, attending Clarion Academy with me! Even though it's Finnian's oldest brother, Farley, who'll be ruling the Warm Seas someday, Finnian is still in line for the throne—Poseidon help us all—so he has to learn how to rule. And there's no better place to do that than Clarion Academy! Foreign royals have been sending their children to Clarion to study for centuries, and no offense to Finnian, but he could definitely use a few lessons. Don't get me wrong—even though his pranks sometimes go too far, he has a good heart, and I know how much he loves the Warm Seas. Still, there's a lot of responsibility involved in running a kingdom.

Knowing Finnian, he'll probably spend most of class trying to propose a constitutional amendment to ban homework. And knowing Finnian, it might even work. He could charm the scales off a sawfish. He even got *me* to sneak out after dinner one time so we could head up to the surface to watch fireworks over the Hills—although I was so anxious about getting in trouble, I couldn't really enjoy it, despite the fact that fireworks are one of the few things land-livers really get right.

Most of my other friends, as much as I love them, don't understand the pressure I feel as a princess. Like I need to be perfect all the time. If they make a mistake, they might get in trouble, sure. But if I make a mistake? *Everyone* knows about it. I can't afford to mess up. The stakes are too high. But hanging out with Finnian is different. He's royal, too, but he never lets that stop him from doing exactly what he wants to do. And as much as I chide him for his recklessness, I have to admit, there's part of me that admires it. Finnian makes me feel like maybe I don't need to take myself quite so seriously all the time.

"What are you guys doing?" Finnian blows a smaller stream of bubbles, ruffling the anemones. I don't think they have

emotions, but I swear there's something slightly peeved in the way their tentacles quiver.

"Talking about going topside," Aarav says.

"Pass." Finnian drops the conch to put an arm around my shoulder. *"Lana and I are going to be too busy learning how to take over the oceans."*

"We're learning diplomacy." I roll my eyes, but I'm laughing. Somehow, around Finnian, I usually find myself laughing at things I probably shouldn't. Taking over the oceans has only ever been attempted by sea witches, and it's never ended well. *"Not oceanic domination."*

"First rule of diplomacy," Finnian says. *"Swim softly and carry a big shell."*

Finnian picks up the shell and aims the stream at me. This time I know it's coming, and I swim ahead of it, letting the bubbles push against my tail and propel me forward, out of the anemone park, faster than I could ever go on my own.

"See ya, Aarav!" Finnian calls as he swims up to join me, conch under his arm.

"Where are we going?" I turn over my shoulder to see Aarav sitting alone in the anemone park, confused.

"Where are we going?" Finnian repeats with disbelief. *"Where are we* going?! *Did I remember an academic appointment that Her Royal High-GPA-ness forgot?"*

I stare at Finnian blankly as I float forward, the rush of bubbles behind me dying out.

"The school visit!" I gasp. *"I can't believe I forgot about the*

tour!" Swimming faster than any conch shell could propel me, I wave an apologetic goodbye to Aarav as I jet toward school.

Because being late for the first day of my political career? Not an option!

CHAPTER TWO

I've probably swum by Clarion Academy almost every day of my life—it's right by the palace—but this is the first time I've actually been *inside*. The big bronze gates are flung open, and as I swim through, I'm half expecting to hear some kind of magical music. I'm swimming through the gates of Clarion Academy, just like every ruler of Clarion has before me!

This doesn't just feel like the first day of school. This feels like *destiny*.

Clarion Academy is built almost in the shape of a U, with a courtyard in the middle and classrooms all around the sides. As Finnian and I enter the courtyard, there are teachers floating by the doors to their classrooms, and future students milling around in the middle. I see kids I recognize from school last year, kids I've known my whole life—the sons and daughters of ambassadors and diplomats, council members and courtiers. Anyone who hopes for a future politician in their family sends their kids to Clarion Academy. I can't hear what anyone is saying in their private conversations, but I can *feel* the excitement in the water. I bob up and down, unable to keep still. Obviously I've been a princess my whole life, but this is the first day of my career as a *real* princess, a political force who's ready to learn how to lead her people.

"Lana!" Two mermaids in the courtyard are waving at me excitedly. They smile as they swim over to me and Finnian, with matching grins on their identical faces. It's Umiko and Kishiko—their mom is the chief councilor at Dad's court. They'd be impossible to tell apart, except Umiko always has her long dark hair neatly braided and Kishiko likes to keep hers wild.

"Can you believe—" Umiko starts.

"We're finally fourteen?" Kishiko interrupts her.

"No offense to Clarion Elementary—"

"None at all, Mrs. Marlin is my forever educational inspiration, fifth grade was transformational—"

"But this is going to be incredible!" Umiko squeals.

I squeal right along with her. After a summer hearing about Finnian's distinct lack of educational enthusiasm, it feels so nice to be around merpeople who are as excited about Clarion Academy as I am.

"Are you two related?" Finnian jokes, looking back and forth between the two of them like he's searching for a family resemblance. It's weird to think that Finnian's previous visits to Clarion were so short, he never had a chance to meet my closest friends here. Then again, if there's one thing I know, it's that when you're a royal, your schedule is never your own.

The twins laugh, tossing back their heads in the exact same way.

"We know who you are, Prince Finnian of the Warm Seas," Kishiko says.

"My reputation precedes me." Finnian bows.

"It sure does," Umiko confirms. *"I heard some story about you and a mariner's astrolabe?"*

"How was your summer?" I ask as I loop my arm through Kishiko's, eager to turn the conversation away from the mariner's astrolabe, which was truly *not* Finnian's best moment. (Nor mine, if I'm being totally honest.) *"I haven't seen you guys at all."*

These past couple months, I've been so busy hanging out with Finnian, I didn't see *any* of my regular friends from school. And now I feel a little guilty about it.

"Weird." Umiko takes my other arm, and the three of us swim toward the classrooms. Well, if Umiko and Kishiko feel like I ditched them, they're not acting like it. Phew! *"Mom made us go camping when the council was in recess. Do you know what kind of stuff is lurking out there beyond the borders of civilization? We saw a goblin shark. Would not recommend."*

"Definitely a hard pass on the goblin shark." Kishiko shakes her head. *"I told Mom that next year, it's a five-star resort in the Warm Seas, or nothing."*

"Everybody wants to go to the Warm Seas." Finnian zooms in front of us, showing off a little as he executes a perfect flip. *"The ocean's premier luxury tourist destination. The cultural epicenter of the entire world. The greatest nation to ever—"*

"I'm sorry, where did you say you were from?" Umiko wrinkles her nose. *"The Deepest Depths, right?"*

"Do I look like an aggressive bull shark from the Deepest

Depths?" Finnian puts his hands over his heart and shoots backward like he's been harpooned—only to collide with a short, middle-aged merman who seems distinctly unamused to be squashed by Finnian.

I clap a hand over my mouth, trying not to laugh. I'm pretty sure Finnian has no idea who he's just run into, but I know exactly what the headmaster of Clarion Academy looks like.

"*Prince Finnian of the Warm Seas,*" Headmaster Crabbe says flatly. "*So glad you could join us for the academic year.*"

"*Me too, sir,*" Finnian says, turning on the charm. "*Truly, what a blessing to be able to sample the educational delights of one of the Warm Seas' most constant allies.*"

"Educational delights?" I say to Finnian, rolling my eyes, glad Headmaster Crabbe can't hear what I don't want him to. "*Laying it on a little thick, there, don't you think?*"

Headmaster Crabbe, who must be thinking the same thing, harrumphs in Finnian's general direction. "*The information session starts momentarily in the auditorium, and the tour will depart from there,*" Headmaster Crabbe says. "*I'm sure no one wants to be late on their first day.*"

"*Of course not!*" I say with my most winning smile, hoping Headmaster Crabbe knows that although Finnian and I are friends, *I'm* at least here to take things seriously.

Even though I was, in fact, almost late on my first day.

Today is the first swim in my journey toward graduation as valedictorian after all—Dad was valedictorian of his class at Clarion Academy, and I won't settle for anything less. "*Come on, guys. Let's go!*"

Headmaster Crabbe remains in the hallway with his arms folded, watching students swim past him. I lead my friends down the hall and toward the auditorium. I had no idea it was possible to be so excited about an information session, but this isn't just any information. This is Clarion Academy information for future political masterminds!

"How do you know where we're going?" Finnian asks as he straggles behind me and the twins.

"Five clams says she memorized a map of the school ages ago," Umiko bets.

"Only a clownfish would take that bet," Kishiko scoffs.

I grin. Obviously, I've had the map memorized since May.

"Come on!"

We swim into the auditorium. There's a stage, almost as nice as the one where the Clam Jam plays every summer. It's about half-full, but luckily, there are still plenty of seats in the front.

"Not the front row." Finnian groans. *"Come on, Lana! Anything but that!"*

I ignore Finnian and choose a seat right in the middle of the first row.

The information session goes by quickly. In no time at all, we're being ushered out of the auditorium for a tour of the school. But before Finnian and I can take our places in line, there's an adult mermaid I don't recognize floating in front of me.

"Your Royal Highness?" the mermaid says. *"I'm so sorry to interrupt, Princess Lana, but there's been a change of plans. Your father has requested you return to the palace instead of taking the tour."*

"Is everything okay?" I ask, worried for Dad.

"Yes, yes, of course!" she reassures me. *"But His Majesty wishes to speak with you and felt confident you wouldn't need the tour to orient yourself."*

Well, he was right about that.

"Do you need me to come with you?" Finnian zooms up to join me. *"You know, for moral support? I'm very morally supportive."*

"Get in line," I say sternly, and Finnian wilts into line behind the twins. *"You need the tour more than anyone."*

Finnian sighs dramatically, waving halfheartedly as I swim out of the auditorium.

When I get to the palace, Dad's not in the throne room. One of the butlers informs me that His Majesty is awaiting me in my room, and sure enough, once I swim to my room, there he is: my dad, the King of Clarion.

"Hey, Cuttlefish."

I roll my eyes at Dad's cheesy nickname for me—I'm not particularly cuddly, and neither is a cuttlefish. He's sitting on my bed, petting Shelly, my turtle, who has her eyes closed as she relaxes. She looks totally blissed out.

"What's going on?" I ask as I take a seat next to Dad. *"Clarion Academy was amazing, by the way. I can't wait for school to start tomorrow!"*

"Ah, yes, well, it's about school starting tomorrow..." Dad trails off, looking increasingly green around the gills. Shelly lifts her head and cracks one eye open, like she knows something's off, too. *"I think it might be best if we started your lessons next week instead."*

"*What? Why?*"

"*Well...if we start a week later, you can go to the Royal Festival after all!*" Dad says enthusiastically, like he's offering me front-row tickets to the Clam Jam.

"*Dad. Come on.*" I start laughing. "*You know I'm not sad about missing the Royal Festival. Trust me. It's fine. I'm fine. I'm happy that I don't have to go!*"

"*Be that as it may...*" Dad looks like he ate a bad oyster. "*It's, er, important to your mother that you attend.*"

"*I have a hard time believing that,*" I mutter.

"*Lana.*" Dad's voice has taken on his addressing-the-parliament tone. "*Your mother wants you there.*"

"Now *she wants me there? Why? She didn't care that I wasn't coming before! You're not seriously telling me she bothered sending a message all the way down here to ruin the start of my school year because she—what?—changed her mind?*"

"*She has a lot going on right now, and I think she wants you to... be a part of it.*" Since when has Mom wanted me to be part of anything? She only wants me to visit *one week* a year. That's practically *nothing*. "*And this will hardly ruin the school year. We'll only be postponing your training by a week.*"

"*A lot can happen in a week! I'll fall behind before school even starts!*" I protest.

I'm already having visions of all the things Finnian will learn without me. By the time I return, he'll probably be negotiating with sharks and orchestrating ceremonial swim meets, while I won't know a bylaw from a barnacle! Just thinking about how far behind I'll be is making me itch like I swam straight into a

swarm of jellyfish. I push off the bed and start swimming back
and forth anxiously.

"That's no problem for you!" Now Dad's veered from
addressing-the-parliament back into his cheerful I've-got-free-
tickets-to-the-Clam-Jam tone—I don't trust this sudden burst
of wild enthusiasm at all. Shelly narrows her eyes, too. *"I have
complete faith in you. You're the best student in the seven seas. I
know you'll catch up in no time."*

*"But I don't want to have to catch up. I want to start on time,
tomorrow, with Finnian, like I was supposed to. And I certainly
don't want to spend my birthday, especially my fourteenth birthday, on land, away from you and all my friends. I want to be in
school. That was the plan all along."*

"Plans change, Lana."

Okay, now I *know* something's off. He sounds sad and very
un-Dad-like, and there's something dispirited in his eyes I can't
quite read. Whether he's acting in his formal role as the benev-
olent and distinguished King Carrack of Clarion, or just being
Dad, he always has it all together, like nothing bad could ever
happen when he's around. Usually the safest place in the world
is right at Dad's side. But at the moment? Nothing feels safe.

"Is something wrong, Dad?"

"No, no, of course not."

He might say there's nothing wrong, but that's not what it
sounds like. Or looks like. I can't remember ever seeing my dad
look so tired, like he's got the weight of all the oceans resting
on his shoulders.

"I don't believe you."

"*Everything is completely, absolutely fine.*" He won't quite meet my eyes when he says it, though. He looks like Aarav when he tells Cook how much he loves her scallop ceviche. (Typical Aarav, he'd rather eat something he despises than hurt anyone's feelings.)

"*Dad. Just tell me the truth. Why do I have to go to the Royal Festival? And why are you acting so weird about it?*"

"*I'm not acting weird. There is no 'truth,' Lana. This isn't some big conspiracy.*"

"*That's exactly what someone involved in a big conspiracy would say!*" I exclaim, frustrated. "*You know what? I'm not going up there. I refuse.*"

"*You* refuse?" Dad repeats, dumbfounded. Disobeying my dad is not how I operate. Finnian likes to joke that I'm so good at following the rules, the Chief of Police should make me an honorary Sea Sheriff.

"*That's right. You said I didn't have to go to the Royal Festival, so I'm not going. I'm staying here and starting my lessons like I'm supposed to.*"

I cross my arms and wiggle my tail onto the floor, like I'm just another piece of coral growing out of the reef, impossible to move. I'm not going *anywhere*.

"*That is absolutely unacceptable, Lana. It is your duty as Crown Princess of Clarion to spend time with your mother—*"

"*Duty?*" I laugh, even though there's nothing funny about it. "*Just like it was her duty to spend time here, with her family? Mom doesn't understand anything about duty. And I don't owe her anything.*"

"*That is* enough*!*" Dad roars. The water vibrates around him, sending little eddies radiating out in every direction. "*This isn't a discussion. You're going, and that's final.*"

I want to protest, but I know that when Dad gets into full-on King of Clarion mode, there's no arguing with him. You might as well try to change the tides.

"*Lana.*" Dad exhales slowly. "*I'm sorry. Let's start over. I know this is a big shock, and I know you're excited about school. But I think going to the Royal Festival this year is actually going to* help *you with school.*"

I raise my eyebrows. Seriously? Me going to the Royal Festival feels about as useful to my academic career as a bicycle would be to a fish.

"*The Royal Festival is the largest political gathering on earth. Kings, queens, dukes, duchesses, diplomats, and ambassadors from all over the world congregate in the Hills every year to forge alliances, make treaties, discuss trade, and maintain the strength of their borders. It's essentially a master class in government.*"

"Well, sure..." Much as it annoys me to admit it, Dad *does* have a point. "*But it's not like I get to be part of any of that. All the negotiating happens behind closed doors, while I'm at the kiddie table with Aarav.*"

"*Exactly. You need a* real *seat at the table.*" My dad pulls out a small box from behind him on the bed. "*That's why I've decided to name you an ambassador.*"

I swim closer to get a better look. Dad opens the box, and there it is: an abalone shell on a golden chain, the official symbol of an ambassador of Clarion.

"An ambassador?!" I repeat, shocked. *"Seriously?! But that would make me—"*

"The youngest ambassador in the history of Clarion, yes," Dad says, finishing my sentence for me with a smile. *"I can't think of anyone better for the job."*

"I mean, obviously, there's a precedent for royal offspring being named ambassador," I continue, staring at the abalone in wonder. *"King Yoric the Young was named as an ambassador when he was still a prince, but he was sixteen, and that was almost four hundred years ago—"*

"And I bet you could swim circles around Yoric the Young. There's no way Yoric the Young knew as much about the history of Clarion as you do. I feel pretty certain he couldn't name every ambassador Clarion has ever had."

Well, I can't name *every* ambassador Clarion has ever had.

Just the most notable eighty-five.

Dad hands me the shell. It shimmers in my hand, quite possibly the most beautiful thing I've ever seen.

"Wow. An official Clarion Shell of Ambassadorship," I whisper, awestruck.

"I had to get approval from the council. The vote, no surprise, was unanimous."

He squeezes my shoulder, and I glow with pride. Knowing that all those merpeople had enough faith in me to make *me* an ambassador makes me determined to be the best possible representative for Clarion. I won't just have a seat at the table. I'll be at the head of the table!

This is the best birthday present I could ever have gotten.

"*I'm especially glad you'll be there this year, Lana,*" Dad continues. "*It'll be good to have someone from Clarion in the Hills. Apparently, the council is renegotiating their treaty with Fremont this year—it should be quite an eventful Royal Festival.*"

"*Fremont?*" I ask, puzzled. "*Why would we care about them? Fremont is totally landlocked. Is that even under the jurisdiction of an ambassador from Clarion?*"

"*Don't discount the landlocked countries, Lana,*" Dad says seriously. "*We may not share a border with Fremont, but the Hills does. And the Hills shares a border with Clarion. So no matter how far inland a country may be, whatever it does sets off a chain reaction that may affect us. Remember, Lana: Everything flows out to the sea eventually.*"

It's one of his favorite phrases to use when talking about diplomacy. I nod my head, trying to show him I understand, trying to make sure he knows that I won't let him down.

Me. An ambassador of Clarion!

Maybe this Royal Festival won't be a total loss.

CHAPTER THREE

"*You're coming!*"

Something very loud bursts into my room. I look up from my books to see Aarav dancing in the doorway.

(Again, people who think all merfolk are graceful? Those people need to take a look at Aarav's dancing.)

"*You're coming, you're coming, you're coming!*" Aarav sings as he boogies haphazardly over to my bed. "*What are you doing?*" he asks, his boogie becoming subdued as he glances at the open books on my bed. When I'm in my room I'm usually surrounded by sheet music, trying to learn or even write a new song. Seeing me buried in books *outside* of the Royal Library is definitely something new for Aarav.

"*Just brushing up on some constitutional law,*" I say casually. "*Figure it might come in handy now that I've got this.*"

I open the box containing my ambassador's abalone, and the look on Aarav's face is *priceless*.

"*Holy mackerel,*" Aarav whispers. "*Is that—is that what I think it is?*"

"Yup." I hand the *box* to Aarav so he can get a closer look. *"Dad made me an official ambassador of Clarion. So I'm not just going to the Royal Festival this year. I'm really going to be a part of it. The negotiations, the trade deals, the treaties, everything."*

"Whoa, Lana, that is awesome." Seeing how genuinely excited my brother is for me is squashing any lingering bad feelings I have about attending. *"When I got the updated itinerary from the Royal Secretary that said you were coming, I thought that was awesome, but this is like . . . extra, super, mega awesome!"*

"Wow, Aarav, that is a lot of awesome." I laugh. But it *is* a lot of awesome. It's almost enough to make *me* want to boogie!

"Are you ready for dinner?" Aarav asks. *"Do you think Dad might eat with us?"* he adds hopefully. *"This is basically your birthday dinner, since we'll be gone tomorrow."*

"Maybe." I don't want to get Aarav's hopes up too much, but it seems unlikely, even on our last night in Clarion. Obviously, being the ruler of Clarion is a big job. My dad has always been busy. But recently, he's been *extra* busy, usually holed up with his council, reading messages from the Deepest Depths, or having endless meetings with Queen Fetulah of the Warm Seas. He never has time to join me and Aarav for Catch the Crab anymore, even though that's his favorite. So family dinner? Forget it.

(People have a hard time imagining the distinguished King of Clarion playing Catch the Crab, but I swear, the man is unbeatable. Don't get him started on That Time with the Japanese Spider Crab That Made for the Perfect Game, or you'll be stuck hearing him reminisce for *hours*.)

"I'll come to dinner soon, okay?" I say, trying to wipe the

disappointed look off Aarav's face. *"There's something I have to do first."*

"Official ambassador stuff?" He waggles his eyebrows, the happy grin back in its rightful place.

"Not quite."

There's someone who won't be as excited as Aarav is that I'm going to the Royal Festival. And I want to make sure he hears about it from me.

If Finnian hasn't already headed back to the embassy of the Warm Seas for dinner, he'll probably be at the shipwreck on the outskirts of Clarion, near the shell-recycling center. After a good ten minutes of swimming, I see the one remaining mast of the big old three-masted ship appear. The anemone park might be where I go when I'm by myself or with Aarav, but this shipwreck is Finnian's and my place.

Something large and metal whizzes over the side of the ship and lands in the sand near my tail.

"Watch it!" I call up toward where Finnian must surely be on deck, flinging projectile pots. *"There are merpeople swimming down here!"*

"Sorry!" Finnian appears, wearing what looks like an extremely rusty helmet. *"Come aboard!"*

"You sure you want that thing near your brain?" I ask skeptically as I swim up to meet him.

"This brain is so brilliant it's rust-proof." He knocks at the helmet on his head, and some flakes of what look like algae growing on top of the rust float away.

How is he ever going to manage school without me? I sigh

deeply as Finnian returns to the rotting chest he's been rummaging through and tosses another old pot over his shoulder.

"I need a favor," I say.

"What's up?" Finnian pulls out a spatula with barnacles encrusted on the handle. He waves it around like a sword, thrusting and parrying with an invisible enemy.

"I need you to take notes for me next week. And get copies of all the homework."

"Notes? Notes? Notes?" he says, like he's speaking a foreign language. *"I'm not sure I'm familiar with this word."*

"Come on, Finnian." Hearing how serious I am, he stops fencing. *"This is really important to me. I don't want to fall behind."*

"Why would you fall behind? My whole plan was to copy your notes."

I blow out a big stream of bubbles. Better to do it quickly, like pulling out a fishhook.

"I have to go to the Festival this year after all."

"Seriously?" Finnian won't meet my eyes. He lets the spatula dangle in the water awkwardly, probably uncomfortable that he's feeling a feeling and not just being his usual sarcastic self. For the first time I wonder if Finnian is nervous about going to Clarion Academy—without me, he won't know anyone there. *"Well, that blows bubbles,"* he says eventually.

"Big fat bubbles," I agree.

"Big fat manatee fart bubbles."

"Finnian!" And just like that I'm laughing—we're both laughing so hard that we're clutching our stomachs, wheezing with laughter. There is *nothing* funnier than a farting manatee.

"*But you want me to take notes? Seriously?*" he asks. "*Can't the wonder twins take notes for you?*"

"*I'm planning to look at all three of your notes. That way, I can get a complete picture. I need you to be the third data point.*"

"*Wow, Lana, no one's ever asked me to be a data point before. I'm honored.*" He swoons, his hand over his heart. "*For you, I'll do it. I'll take these 'notes' you speak of. Good ones. I promise.*"

"*No doodles.*"

"*No doodles?*" He looks scandalized. "*Not even one teensy-weensy little doodle?*"

"*Nope.*"

"*In the margins?*"

"*Nuh-uh.*"

"*Fine.*" He sighs heavily. "*You are such a goody-goody. No doodles. Just plain, boring old facts.*"

"*That's the spirit,*" I say, thrilled that he swam right into my lobster trap. Now I've got a guarantee that Finnian will actually pay attention, for his own sake. And having a third data point probably *will* be useful! "*Can you look in on Shelly, too, please? They'll feed her and everything at the palace, just make sure she's getting enough snuggles.*"

"*I'll snuggle the shell off that turtle. Not literally, of course.*"

"*You're a good friend, Finnian.*"

"*No, I'm not.*" He smiles, the brilliant, toothy grin that gets him out of any trouble he might tumble his way into. "*I'm the best friend.*"

I consider telling Finnian about being an ambassador, but something's holding me back. I don't want him to know that

I'm kind of excited about going to the Royal Festival now, like that might somehow feel like a betrayal.

So instead, I say nothing, and we dig through the rusty pots and pans until we're both late for dinner.

CHAPTER FOUR

One major drawback to being a princess: Nothing can ever be *simple*.

If it were up to me, Aarav and I would casually swim up to the surface, stroll onto land, and meet up with Mom and Grandma and Grandpa and everyone when we were good and ready. But nope. Even getting out of the water has to be accompanied by an extreme amount of fanfare.

I bob in the water next to Dad, Aarav on his other side. Before us, the beach is full of nobility, and behind them, the palace stands tall on the hilltop, flags on every parapet waving in the wind. Ordinarily, this section of the beach—the only part of the coastline within the castle walls—is reserved only for the Royal Family, but with all the visiting nobles here for the Royal Festival, it looks like a carnival. I sigh as I watch Dad smoothing his beard, still concerned, apparently, with what Mom thinks of him, even after all these years. Dad always seems nervous about seeing Mom, like he has to make sure the entire ocean is good enough to impress Princess Hyacinth of the Hills.

Dad and Mom insisted, back when I was seven and they decided to get divorced, that they *both* wanted it—but that doesn't change the fact that Mom is the one who left. Even when they told us Mom was leaving, it was Mom who did most of the talking. Actually, I don't remember Dad saying *anything*. I remember sitting on the edge of a bench in the courtyard at the palace, clutching Aarav's small hand too tightly, refusing to even *think* about crying, while Mom explained that this wouldn't change things.

Of course, it changed everything.

"Can't we just get on with it?" I mumble, dragging my fingers through the water as we float facing the beach.

"What was that, Lana?" Dad asks sharply. Dad has a zero-tolerance policy for rudeness in the Royal Family, *especially* at any official Clarion functions—which this, unfortunately, is. When you live life in the public eye, it's all smiles, all the time. Poseidon forbid the Princess of Clarion look grumpy. And, of course, now that I'm an ambassador, grumpy is *definitely* not an option. A grumpy ambassador caused the Mariana Trench War after all, and that lasted almost thirty years.

Now that my head's out of water, I have to remember to be more careful about what thoughts actually escape my mouth. It's so much easier at home, where I have to actually think with intention if I want someone to hear what I'm saying. Aarav says he sometimes forgets to speak at all on land, he's so used to just thinking what he wants to say, but I have the opposite problem—things tend to tumble out.

Luckily, I'm saved from having to explain my accidental grousing to Dad by an almighty blast of conch shells. (Unlike the one Finnian pinched from the armory, these are strictly musical. No massive forces of bubble destruction here.) From the beach in front of us, the Royal Trumpeters of the Hills answer back, their brass instruments tinny and grating compared to the melodious sounds of the conch. It's kind of cute how land-livers keep building things to compete with what we naturally do better underwater, but it's mostly just sad that they can't keep up.

And that's the signal to go, finally. The Royal Trumpeters part, and Dad, Aarav, and I swim toward the golden dock extending off the beach into the water. All too soon, we're floating right beside the dock, ready to head onto shore. Away from Dad, Finnian, the ocean, the school, my future, my *life*.

"It's only a week, Lana," I scold myself. "And being an ambassador is part of your future, too. Stop being so dramatic."

"Who's being dramatic?" Dad asks, confused.

Son of a narwhal! I've really gotta get my thoughts under control.

"Bye, Dad." Aarav is hugging our father, his head nestled against Dad's broad shoulder. "See you soon."

"See you soon, kiddo," Dad responds.

Aarav disappears under the waves. There's an air lock below the dock, a collaborative project built by the Royal Engineers of Clarion and the Hills—it's pretty clever, actually. The first room is full of salt water, but once it drains, you can open the door into a dry chamber, where we change into human clothes. Then it's up the ladder and onto the dock, and goodbye, Clarion.

"Well, we dropped Aarav off—time for me to go to school!" I dive back down into the ocean.

Before I can make it very far, Dad grabs me by the tail.

"Not so fast, young lady," he says as he gently pulls me back to the surface.

"Can't blame me for trying."

"You are a Princess of Clarion, Lana. And now you're our newest ambassador," Dad says seriously. "I know you'll conduct yourself as such this week. You'll be a true representative of Clarion and a shining example to all of the seven seas."

"Dad." I give him a look. "It was just a joke. I promise." I *know* he knows I would never do anything to embarrass him—or Clarion. Being a princess is important to me, and so is being an ambassador, and so is making everyone in the ocean proud! Even though I complain sometimes about boring royal functions, or having to look happy all the time, I know I'm really lucky. "Stronger than the current," I begin.

"Steady as the tide," Dad finishes the official motto of Clarion and pulls me into his arms. No one gives a hug quite like Dad. "Happy birthday, Lana," he whispers. "Fourteen is going to be your best year yet."

All too soon, Dad is gently extricating me from the hug and guiding me toward the dock.

Sighing, I disappear beneath the waves for the last time this week. The door to the air lock is controlled by what looks like a metal wheel, similar to the helm on a boat. I swim over and grab the wheel, turning it to the left. I pull the door open, swim into the air lock, then shut it behind me, turning the inner wheel back to the right. As soon as it clicks into place, the seawater begins to drain out of pipes in the floor, pumped back out into the ocean. As the water lowers, I sink down, down, down, until I'm sitting on the floor. I hug my tail into my chest, feeling the last of the salt water go. Without the water's warmth, it's cold sitting on the metal grates.

This must be how a fish feels when it's been scooped out of the water in a little net. And, of course, if anyone attempted to come through the tanks except for me and Aarav—anyone who was a *full* merperson—they wouldn't get legs at all. Instead, they'd be stuck here, just like a fish out of water.

Now that the floor is dry, a tiny bit of fresh water is piped in— it doesn't take much to work. I place my hands on the ground to feel the water, and by the time I touch it, my tail is gone. If I wanted it back, I'd just need to touch a tiny bit of salt water, and boom—instant mermaid. Thanks to my half-human status, I don't need magic to change, and I know I should be grateful that my legs just appear as soon as I touch fresh water (I heard some crazy story from Finnian about a girl who got into a whole thing with a sea witch while trying to change her tail for legs), but my legs never feel *right*. Technically, my human half is just as much a part of me as my mermaid half, but when I'm fully human, I never feel like me.

I push myself up to standing and take a few awkward steps

toward the door to the dry room. Just like the outer door, this one opens with a wheel. I turn it, pull open the door, and step over the threshold.

No matter how many times I take that first step onto land, I'll never get used to it.

I shut the door tightly behind me and take a look around. As always, the ladder to the surface leans against one wall. When I look up the ladder to the dock, I can see a patch of blue sky. Aside from the ladder, a mirror, a chair, and a clothing rack, there isn't much in here. Someone has left me a big, fluffy white towel folded on the chair and a dress hanging neatly on a hanger, shoes right beneath it. Unfortunately, it's the kind of poufy pink dress I didn't even like when I was four, and certainly don't like now that I'm fourteen. But even with all the fanfare and the poufy dress, I'm glad the air lock is here. I can't think of anything more embarrassing than being caught changing between mer and human form—especially on a beach full of people.

After drying off, I struggle into the dress, awkwardly bending my arms around to do the buttons up the back. As I work my way through the buttons, the short, round sleeves attempt to smother me, thwacking me in the face. Finally, I make it into the dress, and I pause to look at myself in the mirror leaning against the wall.

The sleeves remind me of two pink sea urchin skeletons stuck to my shoulders. And the skirt is so big you can't even tell I *have* legs—there is so much I will never understand about land-liver fashion. Like why there's a big bow around my waist. Is the bow serving some kind of function I don't understand? Is it an aerodynamic bow, providing wind resistance? I pick up a lock of hair, and it falls limply back down around my shoulders. It's so weird to see it just hanging there, instead of floating around me like it does back home. And the color, normally such a vibrant aquamarine in the ocean, looks dull and muddied. It's blue enough to mark me as different from the land-livers with their shades of brown and yellow hair, but it doesn't look like *my* hair anymore.

Basically, what I see in the mirror is a limp-haired, extremely pink stranger.

But at least there's *one* thing to like here. My ambassador's abalone is on a golden chain around my neck. I pull it out from inside the bodice of my dress and make sure it's resting perfectly in the center of the chain, where everyone can see.

I wonder what Mom will say. I mean, I know it won't be a surprise, since I'm sure she had a hand in planning the ambassadors' official schedules, but it's one thing to know something and another to actually see it. And this abalone is *really* something to see.

I've stalled long enough. If I stay in here one more minute, people will start thinking I passed out. So I grab ahold of the ladder, place one foot on the bottom rung, and begin to climb.

My head pops up above the dock, and there she is.

Mom.

Aarav is standing at her side, grinning, like he couldn't be happier. Two servants, dressed in the livery of the Hills, skull and crossbones emblazoned on their coats, take my hands and help me off the ladder onto the dock. I step toward Mom and Aarav. These pink satin slippers are surprisingly soft and comfortable, but *feet* just aren't that comfortable. Each step feels so heavy, like I've got anchors tied to my legs. I miss swimming. I close my eyes for a moment, trying to pretend I'm weightless again.

"My *baby*!" Grandma pushes her way past Mom and Aarav and squashes me against her chest, the purple velvet of her gown fuzzy against my cheek. She smells exactly like I remember: the sweet perfume of flowers mixed with the earthier scent of soil. I would bet anything she's got gardening gloves stashed somewhere in her skirts. Before Grandma married Grandpa and became Queen of the Hills, she was the Princess of Bloemen, the world's primary exporter of flowers. According to Grandma, even the walls in Bloemen are covered in flowers, like every building is a living, breathing thing. And although she loves to complain that the soil in the Hills is too sandy and the air is too salty for most plants to really thrive, she's created beautiful gardens here, too. Obviously, the gardens are no anemone park, but for land plants, they're pretty good. And since the Royal Festival is always timed to perfectly coincide with the peak of rose season, I always see them at their best. "Happy birthday, sweetheart. I can't believe you're fourteen. My goodness, you've gotten so *tall*," she says. "What are they feeding you down there?"

"Fish mostly," I answer.

"Funny." I feel someone ruffling my hair and look up to see

Grandpa, the wrinkles around his eyes crinkling. "Missed you, Champ."

"Missed you, Champ," the parrot on his shoulder repeats.

"You're looking well, Captain." I salute Captain Beaky, who ruffles his feathers and squawks in return. Grandpa fishes a cracker out of the deep pocket in his long red velvet coat with the golden trim and hands it to Captain Beaky, who snaps it in half.

Because the Hills is right on the beach, the ocean has always been an important part of the kingdom. The Hills has a huge armada of ships that they sail all over the world to trade—with permission from Clarion and the rest of the nations under the sea, of course. But although he may look like a pirate, Grandpa isn't an *actual* pirate. The kings of the Hills haven't been pirates in about two hundred years, since the Maritime Armistice Accord put an end to piracy, but all the men of the court—Grandpa included—still dress like they could sail in search of doubloons at any moment. Grandpa's even forgone a crown in favor of a tricornered hat with a giant white feather.

"Lana." Grandma and Grandpa step away, and there's Mom, holding out her arms. She looks the same as always: hair up in some kind of complicated braid, silver tiara, fancy blue gown. The perfectly put-together Princess of the Hills. I accept the hug and pat her awkwardly on the back. Aarav comes over to join us. I swear, he'll take any opportunity for a group hug. "I'm so glad you could come after all. I am so, so happy you're here."

"Mmrph," I respond, which is not, technically, a lie about

37

being happy to be here—as it is not, technically, a word. It is also not at all the appropriate greeting for an ambassador visiting a nation in an official capacity, but it's hard to be eloquent when you're squished between your mom and brother.

I notice a man hovering just behind Mom's right shoulder. Judging by the crown, I'm guessing he's a king, but he doesn't look like a king. He looks like a dentist. Or a math teacher. No offense to dentists or math teachers, of course, but nothing about this guy screams "leader of nations."

I finally manage to extricate myself from the hug and smooth my dress. Then, most importantly, I settle the ambassador's abalone on its golden chain and look up at my mother expectantly. Whatever issues I may have with Mom, even I can admit that she's not only a princess—she's also a real politician. She's been part of every major negotiation between land countries for the past seven years and has pushed for immense reform within the Hills. I can't wait to hear which proposals Mom has planned for me to present with her this year!

I wait for her to say something about me being an ambassador, but she says nothing. She's not even looking at the abalone, or at me. Instead, she's smiling at the guy hovering behind her.

"Lana, Aarav," she says to us. "I'm pleased to introduce you to King Petyr of Fremont."

I do my best curtsy, even if it is a silly land-liver custom. Dad was right—the treaty with Fremont must be a big deal if the country's king is standing on the dock with her. I can see the rest of the visiting dignitaries, other kings and queens and dukes and duchesses and lords and ladies and all that, clustered on the sandy beach, standing under giant silk umbrellas and lifting glasses of lemonade off trays circulated by servants. Despite his mild-mannered look, maybe King Petyr is more powerful than he first appears.

"Welcome to the Hills, Your Royal Highnesses," King Petyr says. "I'm so happy to meet you. Your mother has told me so much about you."

Somehow, I very much doubt it. But I throw on my most confident smile and try to think of the most ambassador-worthy greeting I can.

"Wonderful to meet you, Your Majesty," I say. "I look forward to our two nations working together."

King Petyr looks sort of confused but smiles right back at me. Aarav pokes me in the side, then whispers, "Very professional"—which is so *not* professional, but I appreciate the support.

"You know, Petyr," Mom says, "Aarav is a real star on the basketball court!"

Petyr?! She's calling the King of Fremont *Petyr*?! It's only my first day on the job as an ambassador, and even *I* know that's not how anyone is supposed to address visiting royalty.

"And Lana is quite the accomplished musician. Guess who else loves music, Lana. Petyr!" Mom says excitedly, like that's such a crazy thing to have in common. "He's in a band!"

I eye King Petyr dubiously. I'm not sure what's weirder: Mom sharing fun facts about me and Aarav, the fact that she's calling the King of Fremont *Petyr*, or the fact that buttoned-up *Petyr* is in a band.

"Oh, Royal Pain isn't much of a band," he says modestly. "Just a couple kings and queens messing around. And a duke on drums. It's hard to find royalty with rhythm."

Mom laughs, even though that wasn't particularly funny.

"They're fantastic, Lana. Especially Petyr on guitar. You'd *love* them. Maybe Petyr can play you some of their songs later."

As King Petyr blushes and stammers, an embarrassing realization dawns. Oh, sweet Poseidon. Mom's not, like, a *fan* of this band, is she?

"Wait a minute—I have an even better idea!" Mom says. "You and Petyr can play and sing *together*."

That is *so* not happening.

"Great idea," I say. "Maybe we can rock out to some sweet Royal Pain jams."

I almost feel bad about being sarcastic, especially when King Petyr's face lights up. He clearly has no idea I was joking. Mom, on the other hand, looks suspicious.

"Ohhhh," Aarav says, like something just clicked into place. "He's your *boyfriend*."

"He's your—*what?!*" If I were still swimming, seawater would be shooting out of my nose in shock.

"Boyfriend." Mom takes King Petyr's hand as the two of them exchange a glance. I stare at their hands like I'm watching a shipwreck. "That's why I wanted him on the docks to meet the two of you."

I'm trying to make sense of what's happening, but it feels like my thoughts are trying to swim through mud. It's not like I need an update on every aspect of Mom's dating life—because ew, gross—but this feels weird. I guess it just reinforces the fact that Mom doesn't know anything about my life, and I don't know anything about hers. When Mom first left, she wrote to me all the time, but I was too mad to write back. And then by the time I felt like there was stuff I wanted to share with her, when I tried to put it down on seaweed, it all felt too stupid and small to be the first thing I wrote to her. So I just never wrote anything. And eventually her letters trickled off, until it was just an occasional update here or there.

And I'm totally fine with that, but . . . a *boyfriend*?!

I bet Yoric the Young never had to deal with something like this.

CHAPTER FIVE

y room at the castle in the Hills has never really felt like *my* room—and it still doesn't, though it's undergone a bit of a makeover since last year, which I have to admit is an improvement. Like always, the double doors to the balcony are flung wide open, letting in the sound of the waves, the cries of seagulls, and the smell of the sea. At least that's a reminder of home. But there's new stuff, too. The flowery wallpaper is gone. Instead, the walls are painted a pretty, pale purple. There's a striped border of musical notes painted near the top of the walls, too. The canopied bed in the middle of the room is overflowing with plush pillows and what looks like a stuffed animal sea turtle. The music notes, the fake Shelly, and the fact that the walls are now a pastel version of my favorite color points to the fact that *someone* is trying to make me like it here.

It was probably Grandma. The national motto of Bloemen is "Bloom where you're planted," and she's spent her whole adult life making the Hills feel more like her home. I know she's always wanted me and Aarav to do the same thing, even though Mom insists that we spend only one week a year up here. This might not be my favorite place, but the fact that Grandma went to so much trouble to make this room more *me* feels almost as nice as one of her flower-scented hugs.

I wonder if my countdown calendar survived the makeover and cross the room to push open the doors to the walk-in closet. Poufy, frilly dresses—so many more pink ones than I'd like—line the walls. I push one in a particularly alarming shade of pink aside and discover that it's still there: my record of the past seven Royal Festivals, little scratches in the paint that mark off the seven days I've spent on land over each of the past seven years. I rub my finger over the last set of scratches, already looking forward to when I go to bed tonight and can add the first tally mark from this year's visit.

Sighing, I head back out of the closet and collapse into the bed face-first. It is, admittedly, really comfy, but as I snuggle the fake Shelly close, missing the real one, I know it'll never be *comforting*. It isn't home.

"Makeover!" Aarav shouts as he bursts into my room. He launches himself up onto the bed next to me, the weight of his body jiggling me. "How *cool* are our rooms now?! Mine's got a whole basketball theme. There's even a little hoop above the trash can by my desk. It's awesome. But wow, look at all these pillows!"

He collapses next to me, and I hear fabric swishing against fabric. I assume he's making a sand angel in the covers.

"Lana." He pokes me. I burrow farther into the pillows, away from him. "Oh, La-na," he singsongs. "Why are you sulking?"

"I'm not *sulking*!" I pop up, offended, even though I'm obviously sulking.

It's not like I thought Mom was going to throw me a parade or something for being an ambassador, but the fact that she didn't even mention it stings. And now I feel silly for wanting her to make a big deal about it, but it *is* a big deal! It's not every day that you become the youngest ambassador in a nation's history!

She could have at *least* said "Happy birthday."

"I know land isn't exactly your favorite place, but look on the bright side, okay?" He sits up, too, squashing a giant purple pillow against his tummy. "Actually, look on the bright *sides*. There's so many good things happening, it's hard to keep track. One: Our new rooms are *awesome*."

Okay, this room *is* awesome. Grandma crushed it.

"I mean, I still wouldn't feel comfortable sleeping so close to a balcony, but . . ." Aarav shudders. Like most merpeople, Aarav is absolutely terrified of heights. We don't have heights under the water. Depths? Depths are no problem. But heights literally do not exist. Which is why everyone is so afraid of them. For some reason, though, I've never found them quite as terrifying as everyone else does. Grandpa says it's because I have "the heart of a pirate," but I don't know about that.

"And two," Aarav continues, shaking off his balcony fear, "there's a welcome party tonight, which you know can only mean one thing."

"Giant cake," I grumble. It's Grandma's signature party move. Every year before the Royal Festival, she has all the pastry chefs in the Hills compete to see who can make the biggest, best, most beautiful, and most delicious cake. Last year, it was taller than Aarav and decorated like some tall spotty land animal with a long neck that I'd never heard of before.

"Giant cake," he confirms. "And three: King Petyr seems cool."

"Cool? Really?" I ask skeptically. "Is that what he seems? 'Cool'?"

"He seems nice, Lana."

That's Aarav. Always ready to be friends with everyone. Even Mom's secret boyfriend.

"Come on," he says. "You're done with sulking."

Aarav pulls me to the edge of the bed, and I let him. Then I let him pull me all the way to the door to the hallway. Aarav is right—I'm done with sulking. I feel confident that none of the past ambassadors of Clarion were ever formally reprimanded for missing negotiations due to excessive sulking, and I don't intend to be the first.

"Race you to the basketball courts," he says. "Last one there is a blobfish!" Aarav blasts by me, running full tilt down the hallway, going so fast he's nearly slipping on the shiny marble floors. On land, *I'm* the blobfish. Aarav always seems so much more comfortable on his feet than I am. But even up here, I can't back down from a blobfish challenge. I gather up my full skirts, clutching fistfuls of petticoats, and plod down the hall after my super-speedy little brother.

We race down the hallway, beneath golden chandeliers decorated with skulls and crossbones and past enormous oil paintings of ships being tossed by stormy seas. All the windows are open, so the sound of seagulls squawking follows us as we run, and the breeze ruffles the curtains, which are all printed with nautical maps of the coastline of the Hills. I pause for a moment to catch my breath next to a mirror shaped like a ship's wheel. Wow—who knew my face could get so red?

"I'm not sure I have time for basketball," I wheeze. "I have to go get my ambassador's schedule."

I can't believe I forgot to grab it right away! But I'm sure even Yoric the Young would have been distracted if he'd found out his mom was dating some king in a band.

"Oh, Lana, Lana, Lana." Aarav doubles back to grab my arm and gently tug me down the hallway. "Plenty of time to pop downstairs, pick up your schedule, and pop right back up here for basketball."

"That's a lot of popping," I grumble. "And a lot of stairs. Don't your feet hurt?"

"Never," he says happily.

I have to watch my feet as they land on each step, always scared I'm going to trip. Aarav flies down the staircase like he's light as a bubble.

One of the smaller ballrooms downstairs has been turned into a check-in area. Milling around in the room in front of a long table covered in paper, I recognize the Marquise de Mertensia, ambassador from Bloemen. And there's Howell Hamblin, the ambassador to Caversham. Wow. It's a real who's who of land countries up here!

I've always found it strange that Clarion is the only sea nation that actively cultivates its diplomatic relationship with land countries. We don't send an ambassador to the Royal Festival every year, but in general, I do think we're better informed about land countries than the rest of the ocean. True, we are the only ones nearby that share a border with the land—the Deepest Depths and the Warm Seas are surrounded by water on all sides—so I guess not every mer-ruler shares Dad's belief that everything flows out to sea. Aarav and I make our way to the check-in table, and I stand in front of two smiling women wearing the livery of the Hills.

"Princess Lana of Clarion," I announce proudly. "Official ambassador from Clarion."

"Your Royal Highness." The smiles freeze on their faces as they shoot each other looks I can't decipher. "We weren't expecting you," one of the women says.

"I mean, of course we were *expecting* you," the other woman says. "We were just expecting you in your capacity as a . . . Royal Highness."

"She's our newest ambassador," Aarav pipes up proudly.

"Just check for my schedule. Please." I adjust the abalone on my chain. "My father confirmed my appointment with the council. Everything is in order."

"I'm so sorry, Your Royal Highness, but we haven't heard anything about this." The taller woman shakes her head. "I'm happy to look through the papers if you'd like, but I compiled the schedules myself. There isn't one here for you."

Suddenly, I'm hot all over. My dress feels too tight, and I can't quite catch my breath. Aarav squeezes my hand in solidarity. I'm so embarrassed I wish I could stick my head in a coral reef and hide there for a thousand years. "I'm sure Mom just forgot to tell them," Aarav says generously. "She's got a lot going on. Planning the Royal Festival is a lot of work."

"Yes," the woman behind the table says. "We will check with Princess Hyacinth, and be sure to rectify the matter immediately."

"There's no need," I say quickly. I'll talk to Mom *myself* about what exactly is going on. "In the meantime, is there an extra schedule I can have?"

"I'm so sorry"—she *does* look sorry—"but I'm not authorized to hand out schedules to anyone who wasn't on the list we were given."

Well . . . great. That's just great. I hunch my shoulders, trying to make myself smaller, wishing I could melt into the floor and disappear. I can't believe Mom forgot to tell them I was an ambassador! And worst of all, since they won't give me a schedule, I can't even drop in on any of the interesting events that are happening! Ugh, this is such a mess.

"It was just a mistake, Lana," Aarav says as we hurry out of the room and toward the basketball court. For once, I'm moving faster on land than he is, desperate to get away from those two women with their sympathetic smiles. "As soon as Mom realizes what happened, I bet she'll get you that schedule right away. It'll probably be there in the morning by the time you wake up!"

"Yeah. It's fine." I brush him off. "I'm not worried about it."

I am, though. The way those two women looked at me, like I was some kind of little kid pretending to be an ambassador, was awful.

And here we are at the basketball court. Ugh. No matter how many times I try to convince him that Catch the Crab is a vastly superior, infinitely more challenging, and much more interesting game, Aarav is basketball crazy. And since Grandpa is basketball crazy, too—he can't play anymore now because of his knees, but he still loves watching games—the Hills has the nicest basketball courts topside.

But as much as I'm baffled by basketball, I can't help but feel happy for my brother. As Aarav pushes open the huge double doors to the Royal Basketball Court, his enormous grin almost makes coming up on land worth it.

Almost.

"Aarav!"

There are five kids our age standing in the middle of the court. The tallest one, a boy with warm brown skin and dark, wavy hair, breaks away from the pack, running toward my brother. He and Aarav hug like they're long-lost besties. I look back and forth between Aarav and this boy, wondering how it's possible that Aarav has a friend here when we only visit once a year.

"Lana, this is Von!" Aarav shouts excitedly as they break out of the hug. I smile vaguely, trying my best to pretend I know who Von is. "Lana. Come on." Aarav's face falls a little bit. Oops. I guess I wasn't doing a good enough job of pretending. "Von? Lord Vondrick Von Smuden? My *pen pal*?"

Oh. Right. I forgot about all those messages in bottles Aarav is always sending up to the surface. Somehow, when Aarav talks about things happening on land, I have a hard time paying attention.

But now that I'm standing in front of him, I do remember Von. I'm pretty sure his dad is the Master of the Horse here in the Hills. Some of the same kids are at the Royal Festival every year because they live here, like Von; some travel with their parents annually; and some only come for Festivals every once in a while. But unlike Aarav, I never really hang out with any of them, so even if some look vaguely familiar, I don't keep track of who they are—something that should probably change now that I'm an ambassador!

"It's so nice to see you, Lana!" Von pulls me into a hug I wasn't expecting.

"Nice to see you, too," I reply, because the Crown Princess of Clarion is always polite. Even when she's being squished in a surprise hug. And especially when she's feeling guilty that she totally forgot about her brother's pen pal.

"Come on, guys. Come meet everybody."

Aarav follows right on Von's heels, eager as a seal pup. Two boys and two girls, all standing on the court, wearing the official Royal Basketball uniform with the big Jolly Roger on the back, turn to look at us curiously. Somehow, I have a feeling they might not be quite as friendly as Von is.

"Everybody, this is Prince Aarav and Princess Lana of Clarion." Von gestures to the two of us. "And this is—"

"Don't they know already?" a short pale girl with curly hair as bright as a yellow tang fish interrupts him. "What's my name?" she asks me, almost combative. "Come on. Read my mind."

Aarav and I exchange glances. He's lucky that our telepathy doesn't work on land, because if it did, I would be shouting the biggest "TOLD YOU SO" of all time into his mind. Land-livers never change.

"That's not how it works," Aarav says, much more kindly than I would have. "We can only hear each other's thoughts under the water. On land, I'm just like you."

The two girls exchange a look that seems to say we're nothing like them. There are so many things I wish I could say, but I bite my tongue. When land-livers go low, we go high.

"Lady Daffodil of the Hills." The girl with the yellow-tang hair extends a hand haughtily before gesturing to the girl at her side. "And this is my sister, Lady Carnation. You'll have heard of us, of course. Our mother is the chief lady-in-waiting to the queen."

If their mom is Grandma's lady-in-waiting, that means they live here, in the Hills. But I feel like I would have remembered talking to someone named Carnation before. As Aarav shakes their hands gravely, I try to hold in a snort. Grandma brought the Bloemen tradition of naming girls after flowers to the Hills, and thanks to Princess Hyacinth, aka my mom, flower names are now super popular. But there's something about flower names that is so funny and stuffy to me. I guess it's not so different from my classmates back home being named Kelp and Coral and Algae and, yes, Anemone—but it feels different.

"And this is Alwyn and Filip, Lords of Hammich and Howard," Von says quickly. "So? Should we play? Three on three, and we can rotate the extra person in?"

"I'm not playing," I say just as quickly, as eager to get out of basketball as Aarav is to get into it.

"Is it because your feet hurt?" Carnation asks. "Because they're not usually feet?" I can't tell if she's making fun of me or if she's genuinely curious. But I'm saved from having to answer by the arrival of a new girl with light brown skin wearing a pink cloud of a dress. Her arms are laden with bottles and snacks as she trots eagerly into the center of the court.

"Gomphrena Baseldon, future Duchess of Quimby," she introduces herself, practically shouting in her eagerness to make introductions. Gomphrena? I have a feeling that must be a flower, but it's not one I've ever heard of before. "Call me Quimby. All my friends do."

"Gomphrena? Did you bring the refreshments?" Daffodil calls imperiously.

"All my *friends* do," Quimby says meaningfully, her brown eyes flashing behind her round glasses. Something about the way she says this confirms my initial suspicion that Daffodil stinks. "No liquids on the court, Daff!" she shouts back. "You're not playing?" she asks me. I shake my head no. "Come on. Let's go eat."

Gomphrena—er, Quimby—jerks her head toward the stands, and I follow her up, up, up each golden stair, until we've made it to the very top. I sit on the red velvet cushion next to her. Wordlessly, she hands me one of the small glass bottles in her hands, with a bright red liquid fizzing inside it.

"What is it?" I sniff it cautiously. I'll never get used to how strongly everything smells up here, but this, at least, smells good: sweet and fruity.

"Strawberry soda. You will love, love, *love*. It's Cook's specialty."

I take a sip, and she's right—I do love, love, *love*. I've eaten strawberries on land before, and this tastes like a super-powered strawberry. It fizzes and pops in my mouth, unlike anything we have under the sea.

"Let's see, what else did I grab?" She starts handing me things from the pile in her arms. "Two-bite brownies. Delicious. Salted caramel macarons. My *favorite*. Lemon jelly sugar stars. Perfect blend of sweet and sour. Oh, nuts, I thought I grabbed the coffee toffee kettle corn, but I think I missed it. I've, uh, got a bit of a sweet tooth."

I look down at all the food in my arms. Even without the coffee toffee kettle corn, we have a feast.

Down below, the game has started. Over the thump of the basketball and the squeak of everyone's shoes as they run, I can hear Aarav's joyous laughter. I'll never understand how he can love it so much up here.

"I cannot fathom how anyone could have that much fun chasing a bouncing ball," Quimby says, sighing.

"It's like you read my mind," I reply.

"I thought that was your thing," she jokes. "Oh—sorry," she says quickly, noticing my darkening face. "That was a stupid joke. I've never met a merperson before. Well, I saw King Carrack's speech at Land and Sea Unity Day when I was really little. But I've never, you know, *talked* to a merperson before. But even I know you don't communicate telepathically on land."

"I'm glad someone up here does," I mutter.

"Apology lemon jelly sugar star?" She waves it in front of my face. "I can't have you mad at me. Your brother saved me from being stuck in a three-on-three game. And now that you're here, I actually have someone to talk to."

"Apology lemon jelly sugar star accepted." I take a bite. It's somehow sweet and sour at the same time, like nothing I've tasted. "Why haven't we met before?" Even though I've only spent a couple minutes with her, I like Quimby right away.

"Quimby is *really* far away," she says. "We only travel to the Royal Festival once every seven years. I was really looking forward to coming this year, but now it seems like it's going to be nothing but meetings, fancy dinners where I don't know what fork I'm supposed to use, and balls where I have to dress up in the itchiest, most uncomfortable dresses my mother can find."

"That's pretty much exactly what it is. It hasn't even officially started yet—from here on out, things only get fancier and itchier."

Quimby moans dramatically and slumps over in her seat. Of course, I'm actually excited about some of those meetings, but that changes none of my feelings about land-liver clothes.

And who knows if I'll even get to *go* to any of those meetings?

No. I will. I'll talk to Mom at the Welcome Ball tonight and get it all figured out.

"So we agree," I say. "Itchy dresses? Unfortunate. Basketball? Totally boring. Lemon jelly sugar stars? Absolutely delicious."

"Absolutely." She nods seriously.

And for the first time on land, I feel like I might have found a friend.

CHAPTER SIX

Nobody throws a party quite like Grandma and Grandpa, and this year, they've really outdone themselves. The Royal Ballroom is absolutely glittering, and so are the people in it. Everyone has come to the Hills dressed to impress. The women are in giant ball gowns and bedecked with glittering jewelry, and the men are wearing richly patterned suits in every color of the rainbow. Although my dress is the pouffiest creation I've seen yet, at least it's not pink. It's silver, with a metallic sheen that reminds me of fish scales. It makes me miss my tail.

I need to talk to Mom about my schedule, but she's been impossible to pin down. Every time I think I see a swish of her blue skirt or the tail of her braid, she's disappearing into another conversation. Obviously, me getting my schedule is a priority, but I also don't want to interrupt if she's attempting a potentially difficult negotiation. That's Ambassador 101. Finally, just when I'm about to lose all hope, I see her take a seat at the center of our table, next to Grandpa. This is my moment!

But just as I stand up to scoot my way over to her, I hear the clinking of a fork against glass. The quartet stops playing, conversations pause, and Grandma and Grandpa rise to their feet as I sit back down, discouraged.

"Thank you so much for joining us at the Royal Festival," Grandpa says in his deep voice. "Although every Royal Festival is special, this one is *extra* special."

This one's extra special? I wonder why. Maybe it's because today's my fourteenth birthday? I sit up a little bit straighter in my chair. I wonder if this is why Mom didn't say anything earlier—maybe she wanted whatever's about to happen to be a surprise! I'm a *lot* less familiar with the customs of the Hills, obviously, but being fourteen in Clarion is a big deal. Maybe it's the same way on the surface, and Grandpa is about to announce that I'm swimming away from the small pond and out into the open ocean with the big fish. Maybe they'll sing for me and bring out fourteen oysters like they would at home, and if I find a pearl, I'll have good luck all year.

Or maybe it's extra special because I'm the newest ambassador! Maybe Grandpa is about to formally introduce me and let everyone know that I'll be sitting in on all the political parts of the Royal Festival! Mom forgetting my schedule will have just been a fluke, something we can laugh about for the rest of my time on land. This is the beginning of my future in foreign diplomacy, an essential part of ruling the ocean's cultural epicenter.

I make sure my tiara isn't crooked and center the abalone on its golden chain so that when Grandpa introduces me, I'll look the part of the princess *and* the ambassador. Should I say something? Probably. I can't believe I didn't prepare any remarks! It's fine. Totally fine. I'll just think of something now. Maybe I'll remind everyone about Clarion's role here . . . something like what Dad always says about foreign relations, about everything flowing out to sea eventually?

"At last year's Royal Festival," Grandpa says, pulling me away from my thoughts, "a trade negotiation with Fremont turned out to be much more than a trade negotiation." A couple people laugh, looking at Mom and King Petyr, who are blushing and staring at each other all gooey.

Well, okay, then. Cool. So this Festival's extra-specialness had nothing to do with me, nobody knows I'm an ambassador, and clearly being fourteen up here is worth sea beans. Which is fine, whatever. Great stuff all around.

"And at this year's Royal Festival, I'm so pleased to announce that—to no one's surprise—the Hills and Fremont will be drafting a Peace and Friendship Treaty! Hopefully this is the first step toward creating a united organization for harmonizing the actions of land nations!"

A Peace and Friendship Treaty sounds fairly innocuous—who could be threatened by peace and friendship?—but as I look around the ballroom, only some of the guests are clapping. For every person who seems pleased, it looks like there are at least two more who are having whispered conversations with worried looks on their faces. This specific type of treaty isn't familiar to me. Maybe I should spend some time in the Royal Library, to try to see if there's any historical record of other Peace and Friendship Treaties. Or maybe some of the other ambassadors will know why people look upset right now.

I glance at Mom to see her reaction, but she only has eyes for King Petyr. Barf. I turn to Aarav to commiserate, but he's looking at them like he thinks they're *cute* or something.

Well, at least we can eat now. I stab my fork into my salad.

"Hey, Lana." I look up, and Daffodil and Carnation are standing right next to me. "What an interesting necklace." Daffodil leans over and actually touches the abalone shell with one outstretched finger. It takes every ounce of restraint I possess not to slap her hand away. "It's very . . . rustic."

"My necklace is an owl," Carnation offers. There's a big golden bird with huge diamond eyes dangling from a chain around her neck. "Did you know a group of owls is called a parliament?"

"This isn't a necklace," I say hotly. "It's the official mark of an ambassador of Clarion."

"Cool, right?" Aarav pipes in happily.

"You're an ambassador?" Daffodil tilts her head. "Are you sure? Because I haven't heard anything about it."

"An ambassador, huh? I'm a Capricorn," Carnation says. "That's why I'm so practical."

"Yes, I'm sure I'm an ambassador." Now I *really* wish Grandpa had said something. Daffodil is looking at me like I made it all up. "Starting tomorrow I'll be part of all the official meetings. The negotiation of the treaty with Fremont and everything."

"The Peace and Friendship Treaty?" Daffodil asks curiously.

I freeze, cursing myself. Why did I tell her I was going to be part of that negotiation?

Daffodil's lips curl into a satisfied smile—she must see on my face that I have no idea what I'm talking about. "So you must know exactly what that's all about, then."

"I do." I look back at her, trying to give her my best royal stare, but I can feel my face getting hot. "Unfortunately, I can't discuss it with you, for . . . reasons of state."

"Reasons of state, huh," Daffodil says, like she still doesn't believe me at all. "Wow. Sounds very real. Well, enjoy your salad . . . Ambassador."

"We're going to pee." Carnation waves goodbye.

"Carnation!" Daffodil hisses.

"Everybody pees." Carnation shrugs. "Wait . . . mermaids pee, right?"

I am *not* going to answer that.

"Have fun with your very real, definitely-not-made-up job!" Daffodil calls as she drags Carnation away.

Unbelievable. I cannot believe she thought I made up being an ambassador! And she poked my abalone! And called it *rustic*! It's official: Lady Daffodil is a total sea witch.

"Did you enjoy your salad, Your Royal Highness?" I jump as a server materializes at my shoulder, already clearing the salad course.

"Well, it was a pile of leaves, so what do you think?"

I don't know who looks more surprised, Aarav or the server. My cheeks flame at their shocked expressions.

"Sorry," I mutter. "I mean, it was great. Very, um, vegetal. Thanks."

"What was that about?" Aarav waits until the server has left to ask.

"I don't like salad, okay?" I snap, my embarrassment at being rude only making me pricklier. "It's a stupid, pointless food that tastes like nothing. Except it tastes worse than nothing, because it's kind of bitter. Haven't these people ever heard of seaweed?"

"Um. Okay. I didn't know you had such strong feelings about salad." Aarav is looking at me like I'm a great white shark and he's a sweet little sea turtle, which only makes me more annoyed. "Are you upset about what Daffodil said?"

"No!"

Yes. Yes, of course I'm upset! This is only the most exciting thing to ever happen to me, and so far everyone up here has either ignored it or doesn't think it's real. I thought being an ambassador would make people take me seriously, but so far it's done absolutely nothing.

"*You* know you're really an ambassador. So it doesn't matter what she thinks. I bet she'll feel really silly tomorrow when you're doing all the political stuff with Mom," Aarav says. "Carnation's owl necklace *was* really cool, though . . ." he adds wistfully. "Come on. Let's go dance."

"No thanks."

"I think it'll make you feel better. Let's shake it off. We can—"

"I *said* I don't want to dance!"

That was louder than I meant it to be. A couple of royals at the table next to us stop their conversation, stare at me for a moment, and then go back to talking. From the way they keep glancing over here, I can tell they're now definitely talking about me. Awesome.

"I don't want to dance," I continue, more quietly, "okay?"

"Got it."

Aarav looks hurt. As he pushes away from the table and stands up, he won't meet my eyes. I didn't mean to yell at him, but I don't even know how to do any of these land dances, and most of the time, I barely feel coordinated enough to *walk*, let alone dance. I'd much rather try to figure out what this treaty is all about—and not just to prove Daffodil wrong.

And I still need to get my schedule!

As I crane my neck, looking for Mom, Aarav heads out onto the dance floor by himself. Slightly self-consciously, he bops his head and taps his toes, grooving alone. Within moments, King Petyr is out there with him, pretending he's got a fishing rod and he's reeling Aarav in like a fish. I'm not sure if that's some kind of stupid merman joke or if King Petyr is just the dorkiest dancer of all time.

King Petyr switches to doing the robot. Dorkiest dancer of all time it is, then. Now Aarav and King Petyr are doing the robot together. They look like they're doing some kind of choreographed dance that they planned out and practiced ahead of time.

Maybe they did. Nobody tells me anything.

I slump lower in my seat.

Finally, I spot Mom, laughing and clapping as she heads out onto the dance floor to join them. Aarav's eyes light up when he sees her. Before we left, Aarav seemed so excited that I was coming, too, but now that we're up here, it seems like he'd much rather be hanging out with Mom than with me.

More and more people flock to the center of the ballroom, forming a dance circle around Aarav and King Petyr. Eventually, the crowd of people is so thick, I can't even see what sad moves they're busting out; I can only hear everyone laughing and cheering. By the time the servers put the soup course down, I'm the only person left at my table. Even Grandpa, with his bad knees, is up on the dance floor, clapping along from the outside of the dance circle.

Soup. Another stupid food. Hot flavored water with bits in it. No thanks.

"Hey, Lana!" King Petyr is now shimmying by my place at the table, Mom and Aarav bopping at his side.

I still can't get over the fact that this is my mom's *boyfriend*. He's just so different from Dad, in every possible way. It's not that Dad takes himself too seriously or anything, but he understands that being king necessitates a certain amount of gravitas. King Petyr doesn't have enough gravitas to fill the shell of a micromollusk.

Does Dad know that Mom has a boyfriend? I think of him smoothing his beard as we waited to come ashore, still wanting to look good for Mom. Dad hasn't dated anyone since the divorce—not that I know of, anyway. Would he be jealous? Sad?

Is there still part of him that has feelings for Mom, even after all this time?

"You ready to boogie?" King Petyr asks.

I am not, have never been, and will never be, ready to *boogie*.

"No thanks." I pretend to be very interested in my soup.

"Come on, just give it a try," he coaxes. I look up to see Aarav nodding enthusiastically at his side. "You've only got legs for the week, right? Might as well use 'em!"

"With those dance moves, maybe *you* should change your legs for a tail."

As soon as it's out of my mouth, I regret it. The dorky smile instantly falls from King Petyr's face. He looks worse than Aarav did when I said I didn't want to dance with him. My face grows hot as I feel Mom and Aarav staring at me in horror.

"Lana," Mom says sharply. "Apologize. Now."

"It's okay, Hyacinth." Petyr places a gentle hand on Mom's arm. "It was just a joke, right, Lana?" he asks kindly.

King Petyr trying to get me out of trouble just makes everything worse. I don't want his help. And I certainly don't want to like him. My eyes start to well up with tears.

That's another thing I miss about being underwater.

No one can see you cry.

But I don't stay at the dance long enough for anyone to see a single tear escape, or to find out if everyone heard what had happened. Instead, I run, as fast as my stupid, horrible legs will take me, leaving Mom to make some kind of embarrassing excuse on my behalf.

Wiping tears from my eyes, I run straight into something that offers up a soft "oof."

"Lana, is that you?" It's Quimby, blinking at me. "You knocked off my glasses."

"Whoops. Sorry about that." I pick them off the floor and wipe my eyes quickly before I hand the glasses back to her. "What are you doing out here in the hallway?"

"Ugh. Daffodil said I looked like a fancy pinecone." She makes a face. I'm not sure what a pinecone is, but judging by Quimby's dress, it's brown and sort of ruffly. "I don't even like this dress, and then I found myself defending it? I needed a break."

"Me too. Well, not the pinecone thing. The break."

"You are very unlike a pinecone. So, you know, you've got that going for you."

Quimby smiles at me, and it makes me want to start crying again. I can't believe I said that to King Petyr. That was so cruel. But I don't want anyone to see me cry. Not even Quimby, with her understanding smile.

"I have to go," I say quickly.

"Are you sure?" Quimby asks with concern as I head down the hall. "Might be worth going back in together for some cake? I heard something about chocolate?"

"I'm sorry—I—I can't!"

A stronger princess would have gone back to the ball with Quimby, apologized to King Petyr, danced with Aarav, ignored Daffodil, and loaded up on cake. But instead, I slink back to my room like some kind of spineless jellyfish and collapse into bed. Shame clings to me like a barnacle. A good ambassador would never have acted the way I did tonight. And I didn't even manage to talk to Mom about my schedule! I clutch the stuffed Shelly tighter to my tummy as I curl up like a little shrimp.

I have no idea how long I've been in bed when I hear a knock on the door.

"Go away!" I call. "Please!" I amend a few seconds later. Maybe I haven't forgotten all my manners yet.

"Lana, it's me." Aarav.

I push myself off the bed and shuffle to the door. Pulling it open, I see my little brother, his green brocade jacket slung over his shoulder. Wordlessly, I step aside to let him in and fling myself back onto my bed. I hear Aarav gently close the door behind him, step across the plush carpeting, and settle himself on the end of my bed.

"What's wrong, Lana?"

"Nothing." Everything. Why is it so much harder to say what I feel on land, where I actually have to say it out loud?

"It doesn't seem like nothing. You're not acting like yourself at all. I know you don't want to be here as much as I do, but usually you suck it up and at least have a little bit of fun. You didn't even stick around for cake this year, and last year you had four pieces!"

"I don't want to talk about it, okay? You wouldn't understand."

"I can't understand if you don't talk to me."

"There's nothing to talk about."

I clamp my lips shut firmly. Aarav's brow furrows, like he's trying to figure me out.

"I think Dad would be really disappointed in you, Lana."

Oof. Aarav's words hit me like a riptide, my stomach flipping in response. This is the absolute worst thing he could have said. Making Dad proud—as both his daughter *and* the heir-slash-future-ruler-of-his-beloved-kingdom—is so important to me.

"Actually, you know what? It's not just Dad. *I'm* really disappointed in you, Lana."

Nope. That was the worst thing Aarav could have said. My sweet, kind, easygoing baby brother is *disappointed* in me? I must have really messed up.

I know I should say something. I should apologize for not dancing with him and try to explain how I'm feeling, and why I said what I did to King Petyr.

But I don't. I turn away from Aarav and curl even more tightly into myself. Aarav heaves a sigh, pushes himself off the bed, and leaves, shutting the door gently behind him.

I know he's disappointed in me. But I can't imagine he could possibly feel worse than I do right now.

As soon as Aarav is safely out of my room, I flee to my closet. Carefully, I put a scratch in the paint right below all the tallies from previous years. One day down, only six days to go.

Worst. Birthday. Ever.

CHAPTER SEVEN

Shelly must be having a bad dream or something. She's knocking her flipper against my shoulder, harder than you'd think a small sea turtle would be capable of.

"Knock it off, Shelly," I say sleepily. "You're fine. That shark is just in your dreams."

"Lana."

Now Shelly's *talking*?! Maybe I'm the one dreaming.

"Lana. Wake up."

I crack one eye open and peer over my shoulder to see Mom, a velvet robe tied over her nightgown, her thick hair resting on one shoulder in a neat braid.

"I know I messed up, okay?" Groaning, I push myself up to a seated position. "I'm really sorry, Mom. I should never have said that to King Petyr. I promise I'll apologize. But can we please talk about this in the morning?"

Given that not even a sliver of sunlight is peeping past the heavy velvet curtains covering the balcony doors, it's definitely not morning yet.

"We'll be talking about your behavior at the Welcome Ball later," Mom says grimly, "but not right now."

Now that I'm more awake, I can tell from her tone that something is wrong. Really wrong.

"Is Aarav okay?" I ask, panicking. "Is Dad okay?"

"I'm right here." Aarav pops out from behind Mom, his voice small. He comes over to sit next to me at the edge of my bed, his disappointment seemingly forgotten in our worry at this middle-of-the-night wake-up call.

"Is Dad okay?" I ask again, more insistently.

"Your father is fine," Mom says. "But there's been an earthquake in Clarion." Aarav gasps. I feel tears spring to my eyes. Clarion, *my* Clarion. My kingdom, the most beautiful, perfect place on Earth . . . hit by an earthquake? "Clarion has sustained significant damage. Countless homes have been destroyed, along with a handful of civic buildings, including your school."

"Is anyone . . . ?" I start to ask, unsure how to say it. "Did anyone . . . ?"

"No deaths, thank Poseidon," Mom says quickly. It's odd to hear Mom use a common mer-phrase, but it's comforting to hear it, even from an unlikely source. Next to me, I hear Aarav exhale in relief. "But the hospitals are overflowing with injured citizens."

"Was anyone in the school when it was destroyed?" I think of Finnian, on his own in a different country. And Kishiko and Umiko, so excited that school was starting. They can't have been hurt. I don't even want to think about it as a possibility. "Or do you know who's injured? Is there a list I can check, or . . . ? You know what? Forget the list. Let's go." I stand up quickly, ready to head to the docks immediately. I don't care that it's the middle of the night. "I'll talk to Dad and find out if my friends are okay, and then I'll see if I can organize some volunteers to help the Royal Physicians, or maybe start rolling seaweed for bandages, or—"

"Lana." Mom stops me with a gentle hand on my arm.

"People are hurt, Mom!" I protest. "*My* people. My kingdom. Clarion is in trouble, and I need to be there."

"You need to be *here*, Lana," Mom insists.

"I am a *princess*. And maybe up here on land that just means wearing uncomfortable tiaras and itchy fancy dresses, but under the sea, being a princess means something." Mom looks at me sharply, but I'm too upset to acknowledge her. "It means that I am always there for my people. Always. No matter what."

"Your people know you care about them. But for your safety—"

"There are thousands of people down there! What about *their* safety? I need to help!"

Aarav watches the two of us going back and forth, his eyes wide.

"I'm sure we can think of a way for you to help from up here."

I snort. Up here, I'm about as useful as a flounder with a sledgehammer.

"Dad won't agree to this," I say furiously. "He'll want me there. As the heir to the throne. He'll *need* me to help."

"Your father agrees that you and Aarav should stay up here until the end of the Festival. We already discussed it." And with that, I sink back down onto the bed, dumbfounded. It is unfathomable to me that Dad wouldn't want me at his side. But if he says I'm staying, I'm staying. He's not just my dad; he's the king, and his word is literally law. (Well, technically, his word is law pending parliamentary approval, but still.)

I have to talk to him. To get him a message. *Something.* My head is filled with horrible visions of Clarion reduced to rubble. Is the palace okay? Poor Shelly... She must have been so confused and scared. I wonder if any of Clarion Academy is still standing. Or the businesses downtown. What about the oyster bar where Dad always takes me and Aarav on special occasions?

What about the anemone park? My hand tightens around Aarav's. Even if the earthquake didn't hit it directly, flying debris could have killed the anemones. My favorite place under the sea, and there's a possibility it's just... gone?

Aarav squeezes my hand and looks at me, almost like he knows what I'm thinking. Like our powers work on land.

"I know it's going to be hard to sleep now, but you should try," Mom says. "I just wanted let you two know what was happening as soon as possible. Aarav, back to bed?"

"Soon, Mom," he answers. "I promise."

Mom nods at him and slips out the door.

"I can't believe we can't go home." I grab the stuffed Shelly and cuddle her close.

"I want to go help, too, Lana," Aarav says. "But Mom and Dad are right. We don't know anything about coral restoration or setting broken fins or anything like that. There's not a lot we could do for Clarion right now."

"Being up here, just sitting around surrounded by comfy pillows while people are *suffering* down there, feels wrong."

"It does. But it's more important that we're safe. Sometimes the responsibility of being royalty is knowing when to take a step back."

A step back. I don't want to take a step *anywhere*. All I want to do is *swim*, down to where I'm needed.

Where I belong.

CHAPTER EIGHT

According to Aarav, being a prince is knowing when to take a step back. But according to *me*, being a princess is knowing when to take matters into your own hands. Which is why I wait until Aarav and Mom are back in their rooms to sneak out of the castle.

As I hurry down the sandy beach toward the docks, the sun is just starting to rise, turning the world pink with the dawn. The light up here is so different from home, where everything is filtered blue-green. I had no idea the sky could be so many different colors and—not that I'd ever admit it to anyone—it's beautiful.

I haven't had this little sleep since Finnian and I snuck up to the surface to watch those fireworks. Hopefully I'll be able to fit a Royal Nap into the official Festival schedule later today—assuming I ever *get* a schedule.

Aarav made a good point about our responsibility, but I *have* to talk to my dad. If I can summon one of the royal servants and get a message to Dad, maybe he'll realize that where I *really* belong is by his side, helping Clarion in its hour of need. In my head, I run through the plans I've come up with so Dad will know how useful I can be. Organizing a roster of volunteers. Creating a list of families who have been affected by the earthquake. Collecting donations to get them necessary supplies.

There's a conch shell waiting at the end of the dock, right where it's supposed to be. I lean over and blow the conch into the water, sending bubbles spiraling down to the depths. One of the advance guardsmen should be here any minute, and he'll get a message to the king right away.

I sit cross-legged, watching the waves roll gently in and out as the sun rises. Almost immediately, bubbles appear before me, heralding the advance guardsman's arrival. Man, these guys are on top of it. But the figure that emerges from the waves isn't an advance guardsman. Unless they've started wearing crowns since I left.

"Dad?!"

"Lana," he says wearily. Dad looks *exhausted*. I've never seen him so tired.

"What are you doing here?" I ask. "I mean, I know I sent out the summoning bubbles, but I was just trying to get you a message. I didn't mean to actually summon *you*."

"I had a feeling you might want to talk." Dad smiles, but it doesn't make him look any less tired. "You have to stay on land, Lana."

"But, Dad—"

"This isn't a discussion." He's busted out The Royal Voice. "It isn't safe."

"It's really that unsafe? Just cleaning up from the earthquake?"

"It's not just cleaning up, Lana. There are all sorts of considerations."

"Like what?" Considerations? I have no idea what those might be.

"Like different ramifications."

"That just sounds like another way of saying 'considerations.' Which also tells me nothing."

"There's nothing to tell you, Lana. It's just more complicated than we originally thought. We had to deploy an impartial investigative team, and it took longer to assemble them than anticipated, and—"

"An investigative team? Why would you need to investigate an earthquake?"

"That is . . . because . . . because marine seismologists don't grow on seaweed, Lana!" Dad blusters. I have a distinct feeling there's something he's not telling me. It's not like Dad to be evasive. I can't believe this. First Mom either forgets—or doesn't care—that I'm an ambassador, and now even *Dad* is keeping things from me? Dad, the one person I thought would *always* take me seriously as a politician. This stings like a jellyfish, and I hate it.

"Stay on land," he says firmly. "Listen to your mother. Watch out for Aarav. Make Clarion proud, Lana."

And with that, he disappears below the waves.

What I wouldn't give to be going with him.

The sun is fully up now. Time for me to get back before anyone notices I've left. I hustle back to the castle as quickly as these heavy legs will get me there.

But as I approach, I see Quimby, eating a piece of cake on the castle steps. My stomach sinks. She was trying to be my friend at the ball, and I totally ditched her. Well. I square my shoulders. I messed up in a lot of different ways last night, but at least I can start making things right. I need to stop being the kind of merperson who would disappoint Aarav.

"Hey, Quimby," I greet her. "What, um, what are you up to?"

"Oh, you know. Working hard to break the cake-for-breakfast barrier," she says, taking another bite. "It's basically a muffin. Let's all just quit fooling ourselves."

"I'm sorry I bailed last night." I take a seat next to her, pulling my knees into my chest. "It had been a weird day. And then I said something I really shouldn't have to my mom's *boyfriend*, and everyone was mad at me, and I just... I couldn't be there anymore." I swallow uncomfortably. "I didn't want anyone to see me cry."

Wordlessly, Quimby hands me her plate. I take a bite. Even the next day, it's still good cake. Grandma really has all the right party priorities.

"I know it's not the same," Quimby says eventually, "but I don't exactly feel comfortable here, either. This castle is about a billion times bigger than our palace. And it seems like everyone knows each other already, and that anyone from Quimby isn't important enough to bother with. My parents keep trying to get me to hang out with Daffodil and the other kids from the Hills, but all they do is make fun of me."

"Daffodil stinks." I hand the plate back to Quimby before I eat her whole breakfast. "Forget about them. From now on, let's just hang out with each other."

"Deal." Quimby scrapes a bit of frosting off her plate, only the sound of her fork hitting the china and the seagulls cawing disturbing the morning quiet. "What are you doing out of the castle this early, anyway?"

"Oh. I was . . ." I can't believe I'd forgotten about the earthquake, even for a moment! "I was trying to go home."

"Last night was that bad, huh?" she asks sympathetically.

"No. I mean yes, it was, but not because of the ball." I squeeze my eyes shut for a second, trying to shake off the horrible images of the school in rubble, the anemones ripped up, my friends in pain in an overcrowded hospital. . . . "Clarion was hit by an earthquake."

"Whoa." Quimby puts the plate down next to her and turns to face me fully. "How bad is it? Is everyone okay?"

"Nobody was killed. But people were hurt, and there was a lot of damage. I don't know exactly how bad, because my dad won't let me come home." I ball up my fists in my skirts. I still can't believe he wouldn't tell me exactly what was going on. Even Dad doesn't trust me. "I just wish I could be there to help."

"I'm sorry," Quimby says. We sit there for a minute, watching a couple seagulls land in the courtyard and hop around, searching for food scraps. Even though we're not talking, it's comforting to have Quimby by my side.

"I have an idea," I say after a while. "When I'm upset, I sing. Do you play any land instruments?"

"I play a little piano," Quimby says shyly, "but I'm not that good...."

"I bet you're great. And we don't have pianos under the sea—I'd love to hear you play. Let's go to the Royal Music Room. This early, it *has* to be free."

But the music room isn't free. As we travel down the east hall toward the music room, I can hear someone playing the guitar. Who could be awake and playing music this early?

"She was so upset." That's Mom's voice. I stop in my tracks.

"Of course she was upset, Hyacinth. You had to tell her that her home had been destroyed."

I'm pretty sure that's King Petyr. Whatever guitar melody he's playing in the background actually sounds pretty good.

"Should we—" Quimby jerks her head back in the direction we came from.

"Shhh." I cut her off. I know princesses shouldn't eavesdrop. Well, *no one* should eavesdrop. But I can't help myself—they're talking about me! I creep closer to the door, pressing my ear up against it.

"She didn't want to come here to begin with. And I feel bad *forcing* her to stay with me, but Carrack said—"

"You're doing the right thing," King Petyr says, his voice soothing. "Carrack was pretty clear that it wasn't safe down there. And Aarav and Lana's safety is the only thing that matters."

We're the only thing that matters? Sure, he had his fun dancey time with Aarav, but all I've ever done is be rude to him. If *we're* that important to him, he must really like my mom.

"Well, maybe not the *only* thing."

The guitar stops. Ew, are they kissing? These are the terrible ramifications of eavesdropping: grossness.

"Okay, now we should definitely go," Quimby whispers. "I did not come to the Hills to hear royalty making out."

"Hard agree. I haven't felt this awkward since I called my first-grade teacher 'Dad.' Everyone talked about it for the rest of the school year. Total nightmare. Let's get out of here."

But as we go to leave, King Petyr starts playing again, and I can't help but stop to listen to the lyrics he's singing.

"This one goes out to Hyacinth; her heart is like a labyrinth—"

"Confusing and deadly?" Mom interjects.

"I'll guard it like a minotaur; well, maybe like a friendly Labrador."

"That does feel more like you."

"Yeah, this is for my Hyacinth; she pushed a statue off its plinth—"

"That statue was offensive." Mom cracks up. This song is kind of funny. And I've got questions about this offensive statue my mom apparently destroyed. "Did you look up 'words that rhyme with Hyacinth'?"

"I've had the finest scholars in Fremont working on it for

a year." He's still playing chords in the background, but he's speaking now, not singing. "And that's all they got. 'Plinth' and 'labyrinth.'"

She laughs again, and Petyr joins in, the sound echoing down the hall. I can't remember the last time I heard Mom laugh like this.

"Come on." Quimby tugs on my arm. "Let's get out of here."

I let her lead me down the hall, mulling over what I just heard. Yesterday was pretty much a disaster on every level, and now I feel even worse about being a jerk to King Petyr. But wallowing isn't going to change anything. Better to just start over today. High tide, fresh start, like we say back home. And the perfect way to start a new day is by committing myself to being the best ambassador I can be. It's time to get involved, for real.

Quimby and I split up when we reach the main hall—she's off to meet her parents, and I'm off to meet my political destiny. With or without Mom, I'm going to get my schedule, and . . .

A piece of paper catches my eye at the end of the hall. It's partially stuck on the leg of an ornate planter—someone must have dropped it. I scurry over to pick it up. Just because there's a cleaning staff doesn't mean they need to pick up every little thing!

Holy mackerel. This isn't just a piece of paper. It's a page from an ambassador's schedule! I don't know whose it is; there's no name on top. All I can see is the outline of events for today. But this is perfect! I can jump right in and then ask Mom about my *real* schedule whenever she's done getting mushy with

King Petyr. For now, I scan the page and find the first event: "International Cheese Tasting for Ambassadors in the Lilac Room."

That is . . . not what I expected. I look closer, and in fine print it reads, "Sample the finest in dairy from our host country and other visiting nations while liaising with your fellow diplomats in a casual setting."

Makes total sense. Dad's always talking about how politics don't just happen in the throne room. And a casual setting sounds like just the thing for a first-time ambassador.

Right. I am *Princess Lana of Clarion*. I am the youngest ambassador in a nation's history. I have *got this*.

The Lilac Room is down the west hall on the main floor and around a corner. Inside, a group of mostly men whose ages range from old to very old mingle, talking loudly, holding little plates. It looks like most of them are frowning. Even though I can't make out any specific words, I get a definite sense that the mood is way too tense for a cheese tasting. It reminds me of the concerned whispering after Grandpa announced the treaty last night. Maybe all the ambassadors are talking about it now? Well, there's only one way to find out. I square my shoulders, take a deep breath, and step into the room.

Nothing happens. Everyone just keeps on chatting and cheesing. I guess it was silly of me to think they'd, like, announce me or something—although that is what happens pretty much every time I enter a room in Clarion. But maybe being an ambassador isn't quite like being a princess.

No, being an ambassador isn't anything like being a princess.

I stand awkwardly near the door, and no one comes to talk to me. I never realized how normal it feels to have everyone know who I am back home. I look around for a friendly face, but I don't recognize anyone. Trying to break into this group of adults is more intimidating than I'd like to admit.

Cheese. I should get some cheese.

There's quite a crowd around the cheese table. I wait patiently for a few minutes, but no one moves.

"Excuse me," I try.

Still nothing. Sighing, I duck under someone's elbow and pop a few cubes of orange cheese onto a small plate, not bothering to read any of the cheese information that's been beautifully calligraphed on a series of small cards.

Okay. This is intimidating, yes. But I can do this! I just gotta get in there and mix it up! I sidle closer to the nearest group. They're the only ambassadors in the room who look like they're having a good time.

"And *that's* why you don't take a spinning wheel to a birthday party in Mataquin!"

That must have been the punch line of a joke, because everyone cracks up. I slip into the circle, laughing along like I thought it was hilarious, too.

"May I help you, little girl?" An old man peers down at me through a pair of spectacles perched on the edge of his nose, blinking.

I almost spit my cheese at him in shock. No one's called me "little girl" since ... ever. That's not how you address a princess.

"No help necessary." I smile up at him like he didn't just speak to me in the most dismissive tone ever. I will be polite if it kills me. "Just here to sample the cheeses and liaise," I say confidently. "I'm the ambassador from Clarion," I introduce myself.

"Clarion? In the ocean?" another man asks, his brow wrinkling.

"Where Princess Hyacinth's children live," yet another explains dismissively.

"Yes. They do. We do. I mean, I do. I am Princess Lana." I tilt my chin up—I consider it to be my most regal face. "Clarion's newest ambassador."

"An ambassador? Are you quite sure, dear?" the sole woman in the group, who's leaning on a cane, asks in a voice that I'm sure is meant to be kind but feels anything but. "Princess Hyacinth hasn't mentioned anything about it. In fact, I'm quite positive she said Clarion wasn't sending an ambassador to the Royal Festival this year."

And just like a gulper eel, I completely deflate.

As I drift toward the door, conversation resumes, like I was never even there. This is *ridiculous*. I slam my tiny plate onto a side table with more force than necessary and leave. I'm finding Mom. Now. I'm getting my schedule, and everything will be straightened out, and I'll start liaising my tail off. And no one will call me "little girl" ever again!

Of course, finding Mom is easier said than done. Unfortunately, this handy-dandy ambassador's schedule I found doesn't include a how-to guide for finding Princess Hyacinth. After fruitlessly knocking on doors for the rest of the morning and sitting through a lecture on Microloans for Major Royals over lunch (I really thought she'd be there for that one!), I finally overhear someone say they saw her heading toward the west wing in the afternoon.

Only one room in the west wing has a guard stationed outside the door—this must be an extremely high-level meeting. It takes all my negotiating skills to get the guard to even confirm that Mom is in there. He won't tell me what she's doing or who she's with, but he also can't tell me to leave. Perks of being a princess.

I've been waiting for hours when my stomach grumbles. Loudly. They've been in there for so long that it's probably almost dinnertime. The hungry part of me wants to give up, but this is the closest I've gotten to Mom all day! I can't back down now!

Finally, the door swings open. As I scramble to my feet, people pour out of the room: I recognize the ambassador from Fremont, and the Law Officer of the Crown of the Hills, and I think the guy with the eye patch is the Royal Admiral of Grandpa's navy? Finally, the last two people to leave are Mom and King Petyr.

"Mom!" I call. She stops in front of me, surprised, waving at King Petyr to continue down the hallway without her. I'm relieved. I know I still need to apologize to him for my behavior at the Welcome Ball, but now isn't exactly the time. "What's going on in there? Is this about the Peace and Friendship Treaty with Fremont?" If it is, the group of people I saw walk out of that room doesn't make sense. "Why is the Admiral in there? The navy doesn't seem very friendly. Or peaceful."

"The navy can be very friendly, Lana."

"Sure, but if it's a peace treaty, then why would you need the military—"

"Who knows better about keeping the peace?" she says smoothly, but something still feels off. I need to find out more about what's going on with this treaty. This feels like *exactly* the kind of thing the government in Clarion needs to know about. And there's one thing I need to be in the position to *get* that information.

"I need a schedule."

"You need a schedule?" Mom asks, surprised. "Really? You've never wanted one before."

"Yeah, well, things are different this year." I touch my abalone proudly.

"They certainly are." Mom's mouth compresses into a thin line of worry. I wait for her to say more, but the longer I look at her, the more uncomfortable she seems.

That settles it. This treaty is about as friendly as a bull shark.

"Oh! Lana!" Mom says suddenly, her whole face changed by her excitement. "I just had the most splendid idea about the Pirate Polo Match. And a special role for you."

"Really?" I'm still not sure I'm ready to let this treaty business go, but the Pirate Polo Match is a *big deal*. It's an annual Royal Festival tradition that could *only* happen in the Hills. They set up an oval track in the middle of the ballroom, and each of two teams has a small boat that's been set on wheels, sort of like a carriage without a horse. The teams race around the track, propelling the boats forward by pushing them along with sticks, and then everyone who's *not* pushing the boat tries to mess up the other team—by any means possible—to keep them from completing the requisite five loops. Grandpa likes to say that the only rule of Pirate Polo is that there *are* no rules. Pirate Code only applies at sea.

But it's not just a game. It has political meaning, too. Each country sends an athlete, and the teams are composed of representatives from all different nations. Grandpa explained it to me like this: When we work together, we float. If we don't cooperate, we sink. Of course, where I come from, sinking is a good thing, but I understand the symbolism.

"Really," Mom says. "I'll make sure all the details are in your schedule. Oh, this is going to be so perfect, Lana!" She claps her hands in a burst of excitement. "This is a part that only *you* could play."

Someone calls Mom's name, and she hurries down the hall. As I watch her go, I can already feel the dark cloud of failure, social awkwardness, and old cheese that's clung to me since I hastily retreated from the ambassadors' cheese tasting floating away. A role in the Pirate Polo Match. Wow. I can't wait to tell Aarav!

CHAPTER NINE

"Okay, here's my new theory: You'll be posted courtside to mediate disputes over contested points. You're so good at conflict resolution. Maybe Dad told Mom about the time you ended the turf war over the Catch the Crab courts."

Ever since my talk with Mom yesterday, Aarav and I have been guessing what my special role at the Pirate Polo Match will be. I wish my schedule would finally arrive so we could *stop* guessing! I suppose I could bug Mom about it again, but talking to Mom would mean talking to King Petyr, and that would mean an awkward apology. . . .

"No way." Don't get me wrong, I love a good mediation, but the Chancellor of the Exchequer usually fills that role, and I don't think they'll be replacing her anytime soon. I turn to look at Aarav, but I can barely focus on him, I'm squinting so much. "Why is it so bright up here?" I mutter, shading my eyes.

"That's called the sun, Lana," Aarav jokes. "Big round thing. Really bright. That's kind of what it's known for."

I shoot him my best withering stare, then quickly change it to a polite royal smile as the King and Queen of Ravanne wander past our picnic blanket.

In all the years I've been coming up here, there's never been a Royal Picnic before. It's nice to have a break from the formality of a regular royal banquet, and from the delighted looks on all the visiting dignitaries' faces, they clearly agree. And despite the aggressive brightness, I'm enjoying chomping on corn on the cob without having to worry about using the right fork.

Behind us, King Petyr himself is grilling meat over an open flame. Mom is hovering at his side, enjoying a glass of lemonade while she chats with some of the nobles from Fremont. Every once in a while Aarav glances over at them like he can't help himself, like he'd rather be with them than with me. But I bite my tongue and try not to act too prickly, even though that stings a little. After overhearing him in the music room, I do understand a little bit better what Aarav—and Mom, obviously—sees in King Petyr.

"Your Royal Highness?" A steward is standing in front of us holding a packet of paper. My schedule! Finally! Before he can even say what it is, I eagerly take it from his hands; then he vanishes into the crowd.

One glance at my schedule and I see immediately that something is very, very wrong.

"So." Aarav leans over my shoulder. "What does it say?!"

"Ship-Shaped Waffles for Breakfast with Grandpa? Intro to Mane Styling at the Royal Stables? Teddy Bear Teatime with Grandma?!" I read appointments off the schedule at random, unable to believe what I'm seeing. "Is this some kind of joke?"

"Tea with Grandma sounds nice." I shoot him a look.

"Pedicures with the Ladies Daffodil and Carnation at the Royal Salon and Spa?! I don't want a pedicure!" I spit. "I'm only gonna have these toes for a week! And the last thing I want to see is what kind of talons Lady Daffodil is hiding under her slippers!"

"Well, what does it say about the Pirate Polo Match?" Aarav asks.

I flip to the next page.

"'The Pirate Polo Match: HRH Princess Lana will sing the national anthem of the Hills—'" I read miserably.

"You love to sing! And you have a great voice! And—"

"'—while dressed like a parrot—'"

Even Aarav has nothing positive to say about that.

"' —and doing a fun little dance'?!" Talk about adding insult to injury! "I'm not doing a fun little dance, Aarav!"

"I'm sure you don't have to!"

"Don't I? It says so! Right here! On the *schedule*!"

I can't believe this. Mom made me some kind of fake schedule, like you'd give to a little kid. I don't want to brush a horse's mane. I wanted to talk about how to make sure everyone has access to health care, and how to take care of the environment, and how to best support our schools! All the things that really matter! Clearly, Mom must have thought that Dad only made me an ambassador as a symbolic gesture to get me on board with coming up here. But he meant it, for real. I know he did.

Then why wouldn't he tell you everything that was going on with the earthquake? a mean little voice in my head asks. *And why doesn't he want you to come home and help?*

I hate to admit it, but the mean little voice has a point.

Maybe everyone thinks I'm a joke.

"Did you hear what happened in Clarion?" I hear a snatch of conversation as two women pass us. "Terrible, just terrible."

"Hardly a surprise, though, was it?"

It wasn't a surprise? How couldn't it have been a surprise? Nobody knows when an earthquake's going to hit . . . right?

"Gotta get some lemonade," I tell Aarav as I hurriedly stand up. I can't let those two women get away without knowing why they expected an earthquake to hit Clarion. "Need it to cool off. You know how it is. That sun everyone's always talking about."

Aarav gives me a bemused wave, and I hustle after the women, following just far enough behind them to hear what they're saying without them noticing me.

"It's terribly unstable down there," the first woman says. Is it? I remember learning about fault lines in science last year, and our teacher never mentioned anything about Clarion being particularly unstable. "All those different nations at each other's throats."

"An absolute political nightmare. If I were King Carrack, I'd be mortified. Really puts our issues with the Hills-Fremont border treaty into perspective, doesn't it?"

What are they talking about?! I'm so surprised, I stop dead, and they quickly disappear into the crowd massing in front of the make-your-own-ice-cream-sundae bar. Why should Dad be mortified? And what nations are at each other's throats? Sure, there's sometimes tension between the Warm Seas and the Deepest Depths about deep-water fishing...and Finnian always has something snarky to say about the Deepest Depths...and, yes, Queen Fetulah's diplomatic mission has been taking way longer than expected...but there's been peace under the sea since before I was born. If that peace was in danger, I'd know about it. I live *inside the palace of Clarion*. The political epicenter of the entire ocean!

And what does *any* of this have to do with an earthquake?!

Those women can't possibly know what they're talking about.

...Right?

But it's not like I can ask a follow-up question. Winding my way through the picnic, checking out the various food stands, I don't see them anywhere. After about twenty minutes of fruitless searching, I pause to watch an elderly woman, dripping with diamonds, throwing little bags through a plank of wood with a circle cut in the middle of it.

Honestly.

Weirdest. Games. Ever.

"That game's called cornhole."

"Quimby!" At least there's *one* person here who treats me like I have something worthwhile to say. I'm delighted to see her standing next to me, wearing a dress that appears to be made out of nearly the same red-and-white fabric as the picnic blankets. "What is with you land-livers and corn? It's practically an obsession."

"Corn is the primary export of Quimby," she says, like she's reciting from a "Welcome to Quimby!" brochure. "But I don't think we have anything to do with cornhole." We watch the woman neatly toss her last bag into the hole, then leave the game. "It's pretty fun. Wanna try?"

"Sure." Anything to take my mind off of doing a "fun little dance" while dressed like a parrot in front of the world's most influential politicians.

Quimby runs over to the board and picks the little red bags out of the hole. They have a funny texture, like they're filled with small pebbles.

"I'm sorry I'm late," she says. "I had something made for you. It took a little longer than I expected."

She reaches into her voluminous skirts—man, I wish *my* dress had pockets—and pulls out a pair of round glasses exactly like hers, except the lenses aren't clear. They're a dark blue, like the deepest part of the ocean.

"I call them . . . *sun*glasses," she says excitedly as she hands them to me. I touch the glass, careful not to leave a smudgy fingerprint. "It was a collaboration between the Royal Optometrist and the Royal Stained Glass Artisan, based on my original design. I thought your eyes might be bothering you, since it's so much brighter up here than you're used to."

Wow. I can't believe someone—a *land-liver*—would do something so nice for me. I put them on, and I instantly stop squinting. I can still see perfectly, but the world is so much cooler and less bright. It feels like being back home.

"Thank you, Quimby," I say as fervently as I can. "This feels *so* much better. You have no idea."

"Oh good, I'm so glad!" She grins widely. "I'm just so happy they work. This is my best invention yet."

"You invent stuff? *And* play the piano?"

"Mmm-hmm. And I kick butt at cornhole." And true to her word, she tosses the first bag right into the hole.

Turns out, my devastatingly excellent Catch the Crab skills don't translate to cornhole expertise, so Quimby pretty much destroys me. But I don't care. After a couple rounds of cornhole, I can't believe I'm about to say this, but I'm actually having *fun* at a Royal Picnic.

On land!

CHAPTER TEN

After a series of humiliating but surprisingly fun losses, Quimby heads out to look for her parents, having promised them earlier that she'd check in. Speaking of family, I should probably make sure that Aarav is doing okay. I left him in kind of a hurry to follow those gossiping women, and then never came back, which was pretty rude of me. Even though I'm having a hard time imagining what kind of trouble Aarav could possibly get into at a picnic, I promised Dad I'd look out for him.

Walking through the picnic, I don't see Aarav anywhere. And once I make it out into the open part of the fields, there's a group of adults playing a game that involves kicking a ball, a queen holding her crown onto her head with both hands as she sprints around the diamond-shaped dirt, but no Aarav.

Finally, in the field beyond this kicking ball game, I see a group of kids. Aarav must be over there, since he hasn't been anywhere else. Something about the way they're clustered is making me nervous, though. Large, secretive groups of land-livers are rarely up to anything good.

I hear the jeering before I see Aarav, and I know exactly what's happening. I pick up my skirts and run as fast as my stupid legs will carry me.

"Look at me!" I recognize Lady Daffodil's high-pitched trill instantly. "'I'm a little merboy, I don't understand pants.'"

"'Do these pants go on my head?'" A pale boy I haven't seen before asks. I can't believe they're doing this to Aarav. My heart breaks when I think of how genuinely excited he was to spend more time on land.

"Put your pants on your head!" Lady Daffodil giggles.

"Come on, little merboy," the new boy taunts. "Pants on your head! Pants on your head!"

"Stop it! Stop it! Leave him alone!" I break into the crowd just as that idiotic "pants on your head" cheer starts to pick up steam. I barrel into the middle of the circle, where Aarav stands alone, looking more upset than I've ever seen him. A thousand thoughts rush through my mind, none of them particularly befitting a princess, or a pacifist.

I look around the circle at these human kids. Most of them are unable to meet my eyes, like they know they've done something wrong. "What in the seven seas do you think you're doing?"

"Oh, I'm sorry, I didn't realize this area was under your jurisdiction, *Ambassador*." Daffodil laughs, making fun of me. "So much for you to do! You must be tired from a busy day of pretending you're involved in the Royal Festival."

I grit my teeth. There's no way I'm going to let her see how much her comment stings. Oh, sweet Poseidon. Mom must have asked her to get a pedicure with me. The idea of Daffodil actually seeing that idiotic baby schedule is too horrifying to contemplate.

But I'd rather turn into a puff of sea-foam than let her know that she's getting to me.

"Is this the other fish?" the new boy asks.

"I'm not a fish. Although I'd rather be a fish than a smelly land-liver. It's pretty ripe up here." I sniff exaggeratedly in the general direction of his armpits.

"Watch yourself." His blue eyes narrow meanly. "I'm the Crown Prince of Caversham."

"And I'm the Crown Princess of Clarion." I narrow my eyes right back at him. "This isn't how a prince should act. This isn't how *anyone* should act. You should all be ashamed of yourselves."

"Calm down, *Ambassador.* We were just having fun," Lady Daffodil says petulantly.

"There was nothing fun about this. You are the *worst* kind of land-livers. Come on, Aarav." I grab hold of his hand. "Let's get out of here. I'm getting land-sick from the stench of these cretins."

I practically drag Aarav out of the circle, walking as fast as I can. I don't stop until we're safely under a tree at the opposite end of the field, well out of sight of Lady Daffodil and the Crown Prince and all their cronies.

"How long was this going on for?" I put my arm around Aarav's shoulder, like that can somehow protect him.

"Too long." Aarav quickly wipes his hand across his nose. I want to tell him that it's okay to cry, but I don't want to embarrass him further. Aarav isn't ashamed of crying when he hears, like, a story of heartwarming animal friendship, but no one likes crying because they've gotten their feelings hurt. "I was having fun kicking a ball around with everyone, but then Von went to go get some food, and as soon as he left, Daffodil and the Crown Prince of Caversham started bothering me about all this stuff they think I can't understand because I'm a merperson. They wouldn't stop."

"Bullies," I say murderously. I never understood why Aarav liked it up here, but seeing him miserable is so much worse than when he was deliriously happy to be on this dry patch of dirt.

"I don't understand." Aarav sinks down to sit under the tree, his back resting against the trunk. I join him. "At home, I always get along with everyone. What did I do wrong?"

"You didn't do anything wrong!" I cry. "And I hope you know that. *They're* the wrong ones."

Aarav nods, but he doesn't look any better. No wonder he's confused. I can't think of a single denizen of the sea Aarav's ever even had a mild disagreement with. Certainly no one's ever bullied him before.

We sit like that under the tree, watching the wind blow through the leaves, until the sounds of the Royal Picnic fade into nothing.

"Thar she blows!" a parrot squawks. "Thar she blows!"

"Well spotted, Captain Beaky." Aarav and I turn to see Grandpa standing behind us, Captain Beaky on his shoulder. "I thought the two of you might have jumped ship."

"No. We were just—" I stop myself from explaining, shooting

a curious look at Aarav. It's not my place to tell Grandpa what happened—that's Aarav's decision. Grandpa might get so mad he throws everyone in the dungeons.

It's an extremely appealing concept.

"Relaxing." Aarav widens his eyes meaningfully. Message received. "Just relaxing."

"Shall we relax our way back to the palace for dinner?" Grandpa holds out his hand, and Aarav takes it, pulling himself up. I push myself to my feet, too. "You know your grandmother runs a tight ship. Wouldn't do to be late."

"Walk the plank," Captain Beaky squawks. "Walk the plank."

"It's not *that* tight of a ship, Beaky." Grandpa chuckles.

Aarav's still holding on to Grandpa's hand. I hold back a little, letting the two of them walk in front of me.

"Grandpa, will you tell the story of the buried treasure?" Aarav asks.

"Of course, of course," Grandpa says. From his perch on Grandpa's shoulder, Captain Beaky fluffs his feathers, like he's settling in for the story. "When I was sixteen, I found an old map, creased and weathered with age, hidden away inside an atlas in the Royal Library. In the middle of the sea, on an island I'd never heard of, there was a path through the jungle, and *X* marked the spot...."

I've heard this story many, many times. I'm pretty sure not a word of it is true. But just like Aarav, I love it anyway. And by the time we're back in the palace, and Grandpa has recounted the time he wrestled a kraken, kissed a mermaid, and found the buried treasure, Aarav is smiling again.

Aarav might be ready to forget about what happened and enjoy his time here, but I can't do that. Once I'm alone in my room, I get out some paper and a pen. Dressing for dinner can wait. I need to get a message to Dad right away and let him know what's happened. Once he knows that Aarav's being bullied, he'll bring us home immediately. I'm sure of it. Even with the ocean floor being unstable, I'd feel safer at home in Clarion than up here with these awful land-livers. I never, ever want Aarav to feel the way he did today again.

Before Mom or the Royal Steward or someone can come to collect me for dinner, I hurry out of my room with my note for Dad, weaving past the nobles mingling in the Grand Hall ahead of dinner to slip out of the castle. In addition to the summoning conch, there's also a bottle at the end of the dock for sending written communication between the kingdoms. I put the scroll in the bottle, plug it up, and toss it into the water. Thanks to a little golden anchor at the end of a chain, the bottle quickly sinks down, down, down, disappearing from sight.

I settle in to wait, wondering if Dad will show up again, or if he's too busy. I probably should have brought a book or something, but I was in such a hurry to get down here before dinner started, I didn't think of it. Instead, I watch splashing off in the distance. Before I can figure out if it's dolphins or something else, the bell at the end of the dock rings, alerting me that someone's posted a return message. Guess Dad's not coming, then. But at least I got a reply. Eagerly, I grab hold of the chain and pull the bottle back up to the surface.

Pulling off the cork with a satisfying pop, I slide out the

message and unfurl the tightly rolled piece of seaweed. In his neatest squid-ink handwriting, Dad has written only one sentence: "Stick it out, Lana."

Stick it out? *Stick it out?!* I had been so sure that Dad would say we could come back home, that he would understand why we *need* to come home.

Frustrated, I hurl the bottle back into the sea and watch it sink down, down, down.

I wish I could do the same.

CHAPTER ELEVEN

How slowly can one princess eat a bowl of cereal? The world may never know, but I'm certainly going to do my best to find out.

"Does it taste better if you eat it one piece at a time?" Quimby asks.

"You really understand the complexities of the dish this way," I reply.

Quimby snorts, then takes another sip from her mug of hot chocolate. It leaves her with a small whipped-cream mustache.

Quimby and I are the only ones left in the Banquet Hall, aside from a couple of chefs tending the omelet station and the waffle maker. I'm supposed to head for the Royal Stables for Fun with Horsey Hair Braiding or whatever Mom wrote on my schedule as soon as I'm done with breakfast. I'm not even sure if I'm really supposed to go to these events, or if she just wrote them down "for fun," but either way, I'm going to make this breakfast last as long as I possibly can. Plus, it gives me another excuse to keep avoiding King Petyr. I know I still owe him an apology, but every time I try to think of what to say, I feel so embarrassed that I can't quite bring myself to do it.

I look up at the sound of footsteps, assuming it's a Royal Stable Hand coming to fetch me, but instead, it's someone I *never* expected to see on land.

"Finnian!" I cry, pushing my chair back and running to greet him, my spoon clanging on the table as I leave it behind. It's so funny to see Finnian on land, *with legs*. He's wearing a long blue pirate coat with silver trim and pale gray breeches tucked into shining, knee-high black boots. Someone who must not know Finnian very well gave him a silver sword that hangs off a belt at his waist. My best friend, armed? What an absolutely terrible idea.

But Grandpa would be proud—Finnian is every inch the pirate prince.

"Hi! How are you? What are you doing here? Your mom *never* sends you to the Royal Festival."

"She did this year."

"Is she here, too?" I peer around Finnian, but I don't see Queen Fetulah anywhere. Finnian walked in totally unescorted. "Where are your parents?"

"Mom finished her diplomatic mission in Clarion a couple days ago, so we went back to the Warm Seas to see Dad and Farley for a quick visit before I had to come back to Clarion to start school. But then the earthquake hit, so they're all busy organizing Queen-and-Royal-Consort-and-Heir-to-the-Throne disaster relief stuff. You know." He shrugs. "The kind of official stuff nobody needs me for."

"I'm sure they need you." I've heard Finnian joke about being "the spare" before, but this is the first time it seems like it might bother him. "Your mom probably just wants to keep you safe on land until everyone can figure out just how unstable the ocean floor actually is."

"Yeah. Maybe. Anyway, here I am, in this unfathomably smelly, extremely dry place." He shrugs, the familiar smirk fixed firmly back on his face. "The good news is, at least we get to hang out more! Like my Gam Gam always says, every abalone has a silver lining."

"Well, sure. No offense to Gam Gam, Dowager Queen of the Warm Seas, but that's less of a profound statement and more of a very obvious fact about abalones, easily verifiable visually."

Finnian laughs.

"And speaking of abalones...it sure is shiny." He puts his hand over his eyes, like my ambassador's abalone has blinded him. "The youngest ambassador in Clarion history. It was the talk of the ocean. Why didn't you tell me before you left? I had to find out from *Kishiko*. She wouldn't stop gloating that she knew about it before I did."

"An *ambassador's* abalone?" Quimby joins us. She blinks at the shell around my neck. "I had no idea you were an ambassador!"

I know Quimby doesn't mean anything by it, but it still stings a little. Yep, that's me, the dancing parrot ambassador no one's ever heard of.

"At least I'm not the last to know!" Finnian crows.

"Finnian, meet Quimby. Quimby, Finnian." They shake

hands. "Yeah, the ambassador thing hasn't been quite the smash success I'd hoped for. . . ."

"Wow. An ambassador. That is so cool." Quimby shakes her head, like she can't quite believe it. "You are *just* like your mom."

"Who—wha—huh?!" I splutter and squawk like a confused seagull. I am *nothing* like my mom.

"I mean, I know she wasn't an ambassador, but that sounds like the kind of thing she would have loved to do at the start of her career. Look at all the stuff she's done just this year! She got King Petyr's council in Fremont to agree to open the doors of the Castle School—it's way fancy and super prestigious—to anyone who wants to go, even peasants. After literally hundreds of years of admission being restricted to the children of nobility. She reformed the prison system in the nearest five kingdoms. And she's even growing sustainable crops on the hills behind the castle—including, yes, corn." Quimby smiles. "Plus, you both have great hair. Her undercut is totally boss."

Huh. When Quimby puts it all out like that, Mom *does* sound pretty boss. But she's a boss who treats me like a joke.

"Yes, Lana, we're all very excited about your political position, but let's focus on *me*. It's my very first time on land!" Finnian rubs his hands together gleefully. "Show me something cool."

Hmm . . . something cool.

Maybe we should go to the stables? At my first Royal Festival after the divorce, Mom tried to get me on a horse, but I refused.

I didn't want to spend any time with her, even though I was curious about the horses. Instead, I spent that whole Royal Festival alternately sulking in my room and learning how to tie different sailing knots with Grandpa in the shipyard. I've never been near a horse since, even though I find myself thinking about them every time I come up here.

But what would *Finnian* think is cool?

Probably the place that's the most like the Warm Seas.

"Why don't we go to my favorite spot in the Hills?" The Royal Natatorium is probably the best part of the whole castle. "Quimby, I bet you've never been there before, either. Come on. You're both gonna love it."

The Royal Natatorium, which would just be called a pool anywhere other than a castle, is down, down, down several twisting, curling staircases, all the way in the basement. Quimby and Finnian follow me, Finnian joking all the way there that this better be an extremely exciting basement. But after I push open the doors, even Finnian looks impressed. Quimby's mouth hangs open as she takes in the scene. The whole room is tiled in silver and black, and the domed ceiling features a mosaic depicting a scene of a pirate clinging to the mast of a shipwreck, frolicking with some mermaids. If you ask me, that pirate looks way too confident for someone who is literally on a sinking ship, and those mermaids look a little too giggly and a lot less fierce than most of the mermaids I know—but it's far from the worst depiction of merfolk I've seen from a land-liver.

The water in the pool is the perfect color of blue, almost like the ocean back home. Through the water, you can see a big skull and crossbones in tile at the bottom of the pool. Grandpa never misses an opportunity to raise the Jolly Roger. Huge, leafy green plants are in pots all around the deck, in between plush lounge chairs, which makes it feel like we're outside, even all the way underground.

The chairs and plants feel like a Grandma touch. If it were up to Grandpa, I'm sure there would be nothing around the pool but planks.

"Choice!" I can tell Finnian approves as he steps closer to the water. "If I stick my feet in here, will they turn back into a tail? All the Royal Sorcerer of the Warm Seas' hard work gone with a magic poof?"

"I wish." I slip off my flats and sit at the edge of the pool, holding my skirts up as I dangle my legs into the water, making sure I don't get my dress wet. Quimby sits at my side, eagerly plunging her feet in the pool. "But that only happens in salt water. And only for people who are half-human."

Finnian joins us, rolling up his pants legs and ditching his shoes and socks. For a minute, we sit without talking, no sound but the water lapping against our swinging legs.

"So, Lana," he asks conversationally. "Why do you look like a disgruntled humpback anglerfish?"

"I do not look like a humpback anglerfish!"

I reach into the water to splash him.

"Now *that's* the princess I know."

He grins, then splashes me back. I splash him, and instead of retaliating, he pushes me into the water. Shrieking, I grab his hand and pull him in after me. From the pool deck, Quimby takes a running leap, then cannonballs into the pool, soaking me and Finnian with a huge wave. She resurfaces, and I hit her with a big revenge splash as the three of us shriek with laughter, the sound bouncing off the tiled walls. Finnian ducks below the surface, then shoots back up, landing in front of me like a breaching whale. I splutter, grinning, as the wave crashes over my face. Finally, Quimby and I team up, soaking Finnian with a nonstop onslaught of water.

"Truce!" Finnian calls. "Truce, truce!"

I stop splashing and hold up my hands in surrender. Quimby does the same.

Mom—and the Royal Wardrobe Staff—may not be happy about what I've done to this silk dress, but back in the water, I feel like *me* again.

Finnian ducks under the water for a moment; then his head pokes out, and he shoots a stream of water out of his mouth in a perfect arc, looking exactly like the little parrot fountain that merrily spits water into the deep end of the pool.

"But really," Finnian says, "what's going on, Lana? I kind of thought you'd be running the kingdom by now."

So did I.

"It's been...harder than I thought it would be, up here."

Both Quimby and Finnian look at me expectantly.

"I dunno, I was just...I was so excited about being an ambassador." I blow a couple bubbles into the water. "But either no one knows I am one, or they don't take me seriously. I'm getting shut out of everything."

"Well, that won't do at all." Finnian shakes his head.

"Maybe you just need to remind everyone that you're here," Quimby suggests.

Maybe that's exactly what I need to do to get Mom to notice me. If she's not going to take me seriously, I guess I need to think of a way to *make* her take me seriously? I don't know exactly what that means yet, but I have to figure something out.

I need to prove to Dad—and everyone in Clarion—that I deserve this position.

"Come on." Finnian nudges me with his shoulder. "Let's shake things up." Shake things up? Coming from Finnian, that could either be brilliant, or very, very bad.

"What do you have in mind?"

CHAPTER TWELVE

"How about these waffles, Lana?" Grandpa says, giddily waving his fork in the air. "They're not just ship-shaped. They're shipshape!"

"Shipshape. Shipshape!" Captain Beaky squawks, Grandpa's feathery echo perpetually at his shoulder.

"They're pretty good," I agree. Listen. It's not that I object to eating ship-shaped waffles with Grandpa. I object to the fact that Mom thought it was the only ambassadorial activity I was capable of.

"Sorry to cut our breakfast meeting short, but I'm due in the Royal Shipyard." Grandpa ruffles my hair as he stands up. "The Admiral and I are taking some of the officers from Fremont on a tour."

"A tour? A tour of what? The warships?" I narrow my eyes. "Does this have something to do with the treaty?"

"No, no, of course not!" he splutters, but I'm not so sure. "No need for warships. Fremont is just interested in boats because they don't have a navy."

Hmm.

"You know, Grandpa"—I leap to my feet, following him out of the breakfast hall—"I'm starting to get the sense that things with Fremont are a little more complicated than just peace and friendship. And honestly, I know a *lot* about complicated."

"Is that right?" We're moving toward the Royal Shipyard at a pretty good clip. I have the distinct feeling that Grandpa might be trying to lose me.

"One time, the Secretary of Agriculture thought a foreign nation was messing with Clarion's kelp beds as an act of aggression. Turns out it was just a confused manatee. I led the stakeout myself."

"Very impressive," Grandpa murmurs.

"So I think, if you just told me exactly why everyone is acting all spiky about this treaty that *sounds* like a good thing, I could actually be really helpful. Sometimes things *seem* complicated but there ends up being a simple explanation. "

Grandpa stops. I shoot him my most winning smile.

"Lana, the treaty is *fine.* It's not something you need to worry about." He squeezes my shoulder. "Don't you have a tea party to prep for, young lady?"

Unbelievable. Why is everyone trying to shunt me off onto these pretend, baby activities! At this exact moment, a Royal Steward pops up seemingly out of nowhere with an urgent message for Grandpa, who kisses me on the head before hurrying away with the steward.

"I don't need to prep for a tea party!" I call after Grandpa's retreating back. "It seems pretty straightforward!"

Clearly, Finnian is right. I need to shake things up.

And in order to shake things up, I need my squad.

First, I find Quimby in the kitchens. She's standing at the counter next to the pastry chef, piping remarkably realistic frosting roses onto cookies.

"How do they look?" She squints at them critically through her glasses.

"Literally perfect. Wanna help me plan some shenanigans?"

"Always."

Grabbing a few cookies for the road—they're *almost* too pretty to eat, but not quite—we go in search of Finnian.

And he's exactly where I thought he would be: floating on his back in the Royal Natatorium, a large frosty glass of something pink resting at the edge of the pool.

"Finnian!" I shout. Startled, he splashes around for a minute before righting himself. "I'm ready! Let's shake things up!"

"Finally!" He swims over to the side and takes a sip of his drink. "I've been thinking about this all night. Lana, you commandeer a warship. I'll grab a cannonball from the armory. Quimby, you're on lookout."

"I'm not shooting a cannon at anything." Honestly. "I was thinking something more fun, less treasonous."

"But I've never seen a cannonball in action," Finnian says sadly. "It's the *one* thing from a land armory I really, *really* wanted to see," he wheedles.

"Lana, what were *you* thinking?" Quimby asks pointedly.

"My mom apparently wants me to dress up as a parrot— nope!" I stop Finnian before he can say anything. He closes his mouth, disappointed, keeping whatever joke he was about to make to himself. Quimby's face is all sympathy. "At the Pirate Polo Match. So I was thinking maybe there was another way I could do something fun. Something a little less feathery."

"Add a little under-the-sea flair, perhaps?" Finnian suggests.

We spend the rest of the day planning. Quimby keeps us fortified with the Royal Kitchen's finest snacks, and at one point Finnian disappears for a couple hours, then returns with a complete set of blueprints for the palace—he doesn't tell us how he got them, and we don't ask. Once she has the blueprints, I'm astounded by how quickly Quimby's able to put my idea into action. She could definitely give the Royal Engineers of Clarion a run for their money.

The day passes by in such a blur that I can hardly believe it when I make the fifth hash mark on the countdown calendar in my closet that night. Suddenly, somehow, the end of the Royal Festival ball is *the day after tomorrow*.

Don't get me wrong—it's been fun hanging out with Quimby, but I can't wait to get home. I haven't gotten any updates from Dad about recovery from the earthquake, and I know Clarion still needs me. Plus it'll be nice to be back in a place where people take me seriously.

Because the next day, at the Pirate Polo Match, *no one* is. And who could blame them! When I pulled on my costume this morning, I couldn't even make eye contact with myself in the mirror.

"I can't look at you right now." Finnian isn't even trying not to laugh. Quimby, at least, is attempting to smother her giggles.

It makes her look kind of like she's in pain, but I appreciate the effort.

"Then *stop looking at me*!" I squawk. Literally squawk. Because here I am, at the Pirate Polo Match, dressed like a parrot. Turns out that part of the schedule was very much real.

Quimby, Finnian, and I are hiding behind the golden bleachers in the ballroom. The Annual Royal Festival Pirate Polo Match is about to begin—and thanks to the three of us, this will be a match no one will ever forget.

"I'm starting to get nervous," Quimby says. She's not looking at me anymore—she's looking out at the crowd. "There are a *lot* of people here."

"It's just a prank, Quimby," I say. "Finnian and I have played tons of pranks before. It's not a big deal. Honestly, it's barely even a prank. It's more of an experience."

"A little under-the-sea flair," Finnian adds. It's basically become his catchphrase.

"I think it *is* going to be a big deal. You know what? Let's forget about it. Let's call the whole thing off."

"Quimby, what are you *talking* about?" I look at her, bewildered. "We've been planning this for an entire day! *You* were the one who figured out how to rig the entire system! You've still got the blueprints in your satchel!"

"I haven't been to a Royal Festival since I was little, and I didn't remember what a big deal the Pirate Polo Match was. I thought this would be more like cornhole or something. This looks, like, *really* official, Lana." Quimby pulls nervously at the strap of her satchel, like it's resting uncomfortably on her neck. "I don't want to do anything that might mess this up."

Quimby looks so upset. What is happening? This was supposed to be *fun*.

"You know what, Quimby?" Finnian says smoothly. "If you're feeling uncomfortable, totally fine, no problem at all, everything's in place already! Feel free to swim on out of here, no hard feelings at all. Lana and I have got it all under control."

"But we want you to be part of this." I smile encouragingly at Quimby, still not understanding why she's freaking out. "You worked *so* hard. There's no way Finnian and I could have figured this out without you."

"Well, actually—" My look silences Finnian instantly. Please.

"I can't get in trouble." She shakes her head. "It's different for you. You're royalty. Even if you get in trouble, it won't be real trouble. But me? I'm just a future duchess from a tiny palace in a nowhere town surrounded by corn. And if this goes badly, then maybe nobody will want that corn anymore. People have suspended trade relations for less. And then I'll have tanked the entire economy of my duchy for—what?—a prank? It's not worth it." She shakes her head again, even more vigorously. "I can't take that risk."

I hadn't really thought about that before. Obviously, being royal is a huge privilege, but it's also easy to focus only on the things I *can't* do without facing serious consequences. I hadn't really thought about all the things I *can* do because I'm the princess of the most powerful nation under the sea, and how that makes things different for me than for Quimby.

"Quimby—" I start, but then I realize I don't know *what* to say. I want her to be here, but I can't deny the truth in what she said.

"And are you sure *you* want to take this risk?" she presses me. "What if it causes conflict between two nations? Do you want to be responsible for that?"

Could this really cause conflict? That's the last thing an ambassador should do. Stressed, I rub my eyes with my arm, then blink as I accidently poke myself with the itchy feathers. Right. Because I'm dressed like a parrot. Something that would never happen to a *real* ambassador. I have to shake things up. It's the only way to get Mom to notice me.

And besides, there's no way I can go through with this song. Or the "fun little dance."

Especially not the "fun little dance."

As I stand there thinking, Quimby shifts her weight anxiously, looking back and forth between Finnian and me.

"I can't watch this," she says eventually. "I'm not going to stop you, but I can't watch."

"Don't let her get in your head, Princess," Finnian says as Quimby turns to leave, struggling past the latecomers still streaming in to watch the match. "At the end of the day, she's a land-liver, too, you know? She doesn't get it. She never will."

I nod, but I'm not sure I agree with him. Quimby's been a good friend, and I think she *does* get how out of place I feel here. Because I know she feels the same way.

"It's just a classic Finnian-Lana prank." Finnian sounds like he's soothing a skittish sea horse. "No big. And besides, it's too late to turn back now."

At the sound of repeated tapping, the crowd quiets. This is it. The beginning of the signal. I guess it *is* too late to turn back, and I'm not sure I want to. I don't know *what* I want to do. The conductor of the band tucked into a corner of the ballroom continues to tap his baton, echoing the rhythm of my pounding heartbeat.

That's my cue. I emerge from behind the bleachers and walk past the crowded stands and the players on the track until I'm standing in front of the band. There are definitely a couple of snickers and also plenty of "aww's," which is honestly worse.

"Please rise for the national anthem of the Hills, sung by Her Royal Highness, Princess Lana of Clarion," the conductor says.

As the familiar sounds of the Hills national anthem begin, everyone in the audience shuffles to their feet. Both teams are assembled on the track, sitting in or standing next to their boats and listening respectfully.

Bubbles start falling from the ceiling, coming out of the sprinkler system Grandpa had installed throughout the castle in case of fire. Bubbles start flowing onto the track from the hose used to clean it. And bubbles cascade into the stands, around the ankles of all the fancy guests. Somehow, Quimby even got bubbles to appear by the band. A giant one pops out of the tuba and floats toward the ceiling.

For a moment, it looks absolutely amazing. Beautiful, even, with the soapy iridescence of the bubbles glinting in the light.

And then the room explodes into chaos.

The spectators start pushing and shoving one another, trying to get off the bleachers. As bubbles flood the track, the polo players attempt to disembark, but the panic makes both boats capsize, spilling everyone onto the track. People fall again and again, slipping and sliding as they attempt to stand up. And from the sound of the screaming, you'd think we'd released crabs instead of bubbles.

"Are we under attack?" A woman's voice echoes clearly above the fray. "Are we under attack?! Is this war?!" This was...not how this was supposed to go. After everyone got over the initial surprise, I thought they would think the bubbles were fun! At home, everybody *loves* bubbles.

I need to stop this, immediately. Stumbling in my parrot feet, I run through the chaos until I find Finnian under the bleachers, standing by the water main.

"Shut it off!" I urge him, flapping my wings with distress. "Quimby was right. This was a mistake!"

"I already did!" Finnian says. "But the bubbles are still coming. There must still be water in the pipes!"

The huge double doors swing open, and Royal Guards rush into the room.

"Remain calm!" the Captain of the Guards shouts. "Secure Their Majesties' safety!"

This was supposed to be funny! I didn't mean to cause an international incident!

"Do you think we should—"

"Go?" Finnian supplies. "Yes. Absolutely. If we leave right now, we can be twenty thousand leagues under the sea before anyone even knows we're gone. I'm pretty sure Clarion doesn't have extradition agreements with the Hills, or anywhere on land."

"No, we can't run away!" I say. "We have to let them know that everything is okay. That nothing is—"

"Captain!" Finnian and I were so busy talking—and panicking—that we didn't notice three Royal Guards surrounding us. "We've secured Her Royal Highness and the Prince of the Warm Seas!"

"Thank goodness!" But that's not the Captain of the Guard talking. It's Mom, racing past the Captain and crushing me into a hug. "Oh, Lana, thank goodness you're safe!" Her arms stiffen around me. "And standing . . . suspiciously . . . right by the water main . . ."

Mom slowly releases me from the hug and looks from me, to Finnian, to the exposed pipes, and back to me again.

"Um . . . gotcha?" Finnian attempts his charming smile, the one that usually gets him out of any kind of trouble with adults, but even I think it looks weak.

"Go to your rooms. Both of you." Mom's eyes are narrowed, and her voice is colder than the water in the deepest depths. "Now."

CHAPTER THIRTEEN

I make the sixth hash mark on the calendar in my closet. Today is over, and that's the only good thing I can say about it. Tomorrow can't come soon enough. I have *got* to get back home.

I've made a mess of everything. I've accomplished exactly nothing as an ambassador—obviously no one here even *knows* I'm an ambassador. If anything, I'm an anti-ambassador, because the prank Finnian and I pulled at the Pirate Polo Match probably just made the land-livers think even *worse* things about merpeople. We could have caused an international incident! Yoric the Young *never* would have pulled something like that. What was I thinking?

A knock at the door echoes through the room.

"Yeah?" I stick my head out of the closet to hear.

"It's me." Aarav. I take a seat on my bed. "Can I come in?"

"Sure."

Aarav enters and gently closes the door behind him. This time, however, he doesn't sit on the bed. Instead, he paces.

"I know I messed up, okay?" I break the silence. "I had no idea everyone would freak out like that. I thought they would think it was . . . fun," I finish lamely.

"Look, I know you like a good prank—and you and Finnian have pulled some epic ones this summer. Wrapping the throne room in seaweed? Hilarious. Filling my bed with starfish? I wasn't even mad. You got me! But the Lana I know would never *ever* do something to disrupt a royal event," Aarav says. "She always represents her people proudly, no matter where she is or what she's doing. I mean, come on, Lana. You're the only person who managed to stay awake and smiling during that Salute to Sea Slugs parade."

That *was* incredibly boring. But when I'm doing stuff for Clarion, it always feels worth it to put my best fin forward, no matter how many sea slugs I have to wave at.

"It's different up here. You know what these land-livers are like. All they do is make fun of us!"

"Some of them . . . haven't been great," he admits. "But you don't punish the whole school because of a few rotten fish. The Pirate Polo Match is really important. With all those different countries involved, this could have been really bad for the Hills. And Clarion, too!" Great. Even my little brother has a better head for foreign policy than I do. "And you know that event is Grandpa's favorite part of the Royal Festival. He looks forward to it every year."

Of course he does. And now he has to go a whole year without it. Because of *me*. Why didn't I think about that?

But instead of admitting how bad I feel, I just mutter, "It was supposed to be a joke."

The look Aarav shoots me is so filled with disappointment, I have to look away. The fact that I've let him down is crushing me, almost like it's a physical thing, taking up too much space in this room.

"I feel like you're becoming another person," Aarav says eventually. "Another person who . . . well, another person."

He couldn't bring himself to finish his sentence, but what he meant is clear enough: another person he doesn't like very much.

"I'm still me," I whisper, but I don't know if he heard it. Why is it so hard for me to apologize—to admit that I've been wrong? I wish I hadn't pulled this stupid prank at all, but unfortunately, I can't go back and undo it. No Royal Sorcerer has cracked time travel yet.

When I finally look up, Aarav is gone, the door shut behind him.

My face is wet. Usually, my face is wet for all the right reasons—like I'm at home, swimming—but not today. I touch my hands to my cheeks, surprised to find myself crying. I hate crying. I almost *never* do it. It makes me feel not like *me*, like my emotions are too big for my body and I can't control them. And I hate not feeling like I'm in control of things. A princess is *always* supposed to be in control: not just of her kingdom, but of herself, too.

Furiously, I wipe the backs of my hands across my face, but that doesn't stop the tears. Aarav being disappointed in me is the worst feeling ever. All I've done since we got up here is disappoint him, and it just keeps getting worse and worse.

Another knock at the door.

Awesome. Who's up next on the Let's-Make-Lana-Feel-Terrible Tour?

"Yeah?" I call, wiping my face off with a corner of my blanket.

"It's Mom," she answers. "Can I come in?"

"Fine." Why not? There's nothing she can say that could possibly make me feel worse than Aarav has.

Mom stands in the same place Aarav did, staring, disappointed. I stare back. Right now, I can really see the family resemblance between Aarav and Mom. If this wasn't such a nightmare, it would almost be funny.

"I'm beyond disappointed in you, Lana," Mom says. "Releasing bubbles into a crowded room? A room that included people in unstable, wheeled boats on a slippery track? That was reckless. Someone could have gotten seriously hurt."

"No, they couldn't have!" I counter. "We specifically set the bubbles to go off *before* the match started so it wouldn't mess with the boats."

"But it *did* mess with the boats. They both capsized. Did you see how many people tumbled onto the track? And regardless of what happened to the players, everyone in the stands started pushing and shoving as they tried to leave. Old Dame Miranda of Farfallen got bumped in the scuffle and fell—she could have broken another hip!"

"I didn't intend to break any old ladies' hips!" I protest. "Obviously!"

"It's not always about what you *intend* to do. Even if your intentions were good—which, in this case, I'm not sure they were—"

I open my mouth to protest, but Mom silences me with a look, holding up her hand for quiet, and I let her continue.

"Sometimes the outcome matters more than the intention. We're royalty, Lana. We can't afford to be careless. That's part of our responsibility."

"Like you know so much about responsibility," I say under my breath.

I don't know if she didn't hear me or she's choosing not to, but she doesn't respond. Seriously. What a hypocrite. *She* wants to talk about responsibility?! She's the one who *abandoned* her family. That's kind of a big responsibility to just, you know, decide you don't really care about anymore.

I used to try to understand how Mom could leave. Once the anger cleared a little, I tried to imagine how I would feel, if I *somehow* fell in love with a land-liver and moved ashore. Could I give up a life underwater?

I couldn't. The ocean is home, and I can't imagine falling in love could ever be more powerful than the pull of the waves.

But Mom *chose* to live under the sea. She made the decision knowing what she was giving up, and she should have stuck with it. Because *responsibility*.

"This wasn't a good time for a prank." Mom rubs her temples wearily. "It's been a very tense Royal Festival. Many of the other land countries have voiced strong objections to the Hills-Fremont Treaty. By the time they're done making adjustments, I'm not sure there'll be any treaty left."

"Why?" This treaty has never made any sense. "Who would object to a Peace and Friendship Treaty?"

"When you take the throne yourself, Lana, you'll come to find that most sovereigns object to anything that could possibly be perceived as a threat. Even if it's something that you *know* could never hurt anyone."

A threat. I still don't understand. Everyone should want peace . . . right?

Well, there's only one way I can *really* understand. I'll ask her if I can go with her to at least one meeting before we head home tomorrow, like a *real* ambassador would. That way this Royal Festival won't have been a total waste. Maybe I'll—

"And then the Royal Guards caught the Quimby girl with the castle blueprints in her satchel, which only made matters worse. It took quite a bit of work to convince certain military-minded parties that the region's smallest duchy hadn't sent a fourteen-year-old girl to commit an act of espionage."

"I'm sorry—they *what*?" Quimby left before we did anything. She tried to talk us out of it. How could this have happened?

"Quimby's not planning anything!" I continue. "I mean, yes, she had the blueprints, but that was just for the bubbles. Not espionage. And she tried to stop us. So—"

"The duchy of Quimby has been issued a formal reprimand. They'll be allowed to stay for the farewell brunch tomorrow, but the council has yet to decide whether or not they'll be invited back to future Royal Festivals."

This is exactly what Quimby was afraid of. I can't believe I got her involved in this mess. And I didn't just get my friend in trouble—I got an entire *duchy* in trouble!

"There's something else I came to talk to you about," Mom

says while I'm still spinning out about Quimby. I brace myself, waiting for her to tell me that the king of some powerful allied country has a debilitating bubble allergy. She takes a seat next to me on the bed and lifts her hand, like she's going to take mine. But her hand hovers, then drops awkwardly to her side. "I know the Festival ends tomorrow, but you won't be going home then."

I freeze, my arms stiffening at my sides, as Mom shoots me an intense gaze, almost like she's looking for something.

Won't be going home?

That's not possible.

I've kept the countdown calendar faithfully every day. There's no way I messed it up.

I need to go home. I *have* to.

"I don't understand." I *don't* understand. Even with the earthquake, staying here for longer than the Festival was never part of the plan.

"I've just received a letter from your father, asking me to keep you and your brother up here longer."

"That's not possible," I say. Longer? I can't stay longer! I've already been up here for way *too* long! I can't make it another day, let alone survive an unknown, possibly never-ending length of time! "Show me the letter."

"Lana." Mom looks hurt, like she can't believe I'd dare to ask for proof. But who would blame me for being suspicious? This doesn't sound like Dad at all. No matter how busy he is, he always wants me at his side. Or at least, I thought he did. "I wouldn't lie to you."

"Show me the letter. *Please.*" I'm practically begging.

Mom reaches into the pocket of her gown and hands over a seaweed scroll. I unroll it and scan it briefly. Yup, that's Dad's handwriting for sure. Asking Mom to keep us here longer.

I can't believe he would do this to me.

When bad things happen, I've heard people say they felt crushed before, but now I really understand what it means. It's almost like my insides have literally been crushed, like they're collapsing as I feel this horrible pit deep, deep down in my stomach.

"I know this isn't the news you hoped for—"

"*Hoped* for?" I repeat back to her. "'Hope' isn't strong enough of a word! All I *dream* about is getting to escape this horrible place. I hate it here!" I shout. "And I hate *you!*" Mom's face crumples, but I can't stop shouting. I'm too angry. "And I don't understand why my father doesn't want me to come home! He's supposed to be the one who *wants* me! Unlike *you!*"

"Oh, Lana." Now Mom's face is really crumpled, her eyebrows knit together, her eyes filling with tears. "Is that what you think? That I don't want you?"

"It's pretty obvious!"

"Of course I want you! I just—"

"Stop lying!" I interrupt her. I'm shouting and crying at the same time, all these horrible, ugly emotions spewing out of me, like I'm a submarine volcano instead of a princess. The normally composed, confident Lana wouldn't even recognize me now. "You didn't want me seven years ago, and you don't want me now. So why don't you get away from me, like you've always been so desperate to do!"

"Lana, I—"

Mom looks destroyed. But I don't care. I can't spend another minute with her. I just want her gone.

"Go!" I shout.

"Lana," she protests again.

"Go, okay? Just leave!" I'm really crying now, so hard I wonder if Mom can even understand what I'm saying. "Just leave. Please."

Finally, she does.

And I'm alone like I wanted to be . . . but I've never felt worse.

CHAPTER FOURTEEN

The Farewell Brunch is the final event of the Royal Festival. I wanted to skip it, believe me. I actually kind of thought Mom would insist I stay in my room, and I was sort of looking forward to my grounding so I wouldn't have to face anyone. But instead, she sent one of her ladies-in-waiting to bring me down to brunch, so I could sit here, smiling at my waffles, pretending I didn't spend last night crying and screaming. Sometimes the worst punishment is no punishment at all.

Well, that's royal life for you. Keep up appearances at all costs.

Although my seat at the head table is officially supposed to be next to Mom and Aarav, right now I'm sitting in between two empty chairs. Aarav is nowhere to be seen, but Mom and King Petyr are working the room, going from table to table as they thank their guests for coming. Right now, they're talking to two women wearing glasses. King Petyr shifts his weight, putting his arm around Mom, and now I can see there's a third person at the table.

It's Quimby.

Quimby pauses with her fork halfway to her mouth as we make eye contact. I wave her over, suddenly wishing desperately that we could talk. I'll apologize for getting her in trouble and promise her that I'll do everything I can to make sure her duchy isn't banned from the Royal Festival, and then we can hang out one last time. But she doesn't come over. Instead, she takes a bite of her waffles, chews, swallows, and looks back down, like I don't even exist.

Ouch. I know I probably deserve that, but it still stings. Today is her last day here, and she won't even say goodbye. I can't believe this is how we're ending things. The temptation to smush my face into my waffles and try to shut off my senses to everything but the scent of maple syrup is strong, but I'm too queasy to take another bite.

Even if maple syrup is the most delicious substance on land.

Finally, I spot Aarav. He's over at the waffle bar, smiling as the chef puts an absolute tower of whipped cream on top of his waffle stack. Eventually, he makes his way over to me and silently slides into a chair.

I can't meet his eyes. I'm ashamed of how I acted yesterday, and I'm scared that if I actually look at him, I'll start crying again. Instead, I watch Quimby and her family get up and go, their heads held high even as the other visiting dignitaries deliberately avoid eye contact, or huddle in close to whisper about them.

And it's all my fault.

"Is it just me," Aarav says, "or does it feel like this Royal Festival has been a bit longer than usual?"

I look up and burst out laughing. He's covered his eyebrows in whipped cream and given himself a whipped cream beard and mustache, too, so he looks like Nereus, the old man of the sea.

"It's been eighty-four years," he says in a tremulous old-man voice.

I pull him into a hug, laughing, not even caring about the whipped cream I get on my shoulder.

"Okay, even *I* don't think it's been that long," I say. "And I thought you were having a good time up here."

"I am. Mostly. But I can tell it's making you miserable, Lana. And I don't want you to be miserable. You're my favorite person in the whole world."

"Still?" I ask, remembering how awful last night was.

"Always," he replies.

I don't deserve Aarav's kindness. I never have. But that's my little brother. He's probably already forgiven those horrible kids who were bullying him. On the bright side, hopefully most of them have left now that the Royal Festival is over, heading back to whatever putrid kingdoms they slithered out of. Good riddance. I'm still stuck with Daffodil, since she lives here, but getting rid of *some* of them takes a bit of the sting out of Quimby leaving without saying goodbye.

"Hey, Mom," Aarav says. I look over my shoulder to see Mom standing behind her chair, her back to me.

"Aarav!" Mom exclaims, practically jumping out of her skin

as she turns around, one hand pressed against her chest like she's trying to calm a racing heart. "Goodness. You...um... startled me."

"Sorry?" Aarav looks confused. I am, too.

"Nothing to be sorry about." Her eyes dart nervously from Aarav to me to Aarav and back again. "And Lana. Here you are. Everything...seems...normal?"

She's searching my eyes like she's looking for something. Probably an apology. But it's not coming. I do feel a little bad about how crushed she seemed last night, but it doesn't change the fact that I meant what I said. She acted like she doesn't want us, and she hasn't done anything to convince me otherwise.

"Yep. All normal." I still hate it up here—what could be more normal than that?

"Good. Great. Excellent. Oh, would you look at that?" Mom is frantically waving at someone across the room. Aarav and I follow her gaze, but there is no one waving back. No one is even looking at her. "Looks like I have to...I simply must... if you'll excuse me."

Mom books it across the room like the Saltstraumen Maelstrom is at her back. But there's no current propelling her—only her desire to get away from us as soon as possible. Because that's what she does. She leaves.

If she's trying to convince me she *does* want us here, she's not doing a great job.

"Do you think she's okay?" Aarav asks as soon as Mom is out of earshot. "She seems...weird, right?"

"I think she's just sick of having us around." I watch her

return to working her way around the room with King Petyr, the two of them making effortless conversation. It looks like she knows every single person here—probably hundreds of royal guests—by name. I grudgingly remember how Dad always says that you need to remember the personal element of the political—even I have to admit that Mom does that well. "She probably can't wait to get rid of us. I'm sure she's watching the waves every morning, waiting for news from Dad that it's time for us to go back."

"Don't say that, Lana. Mom loves us. She doesn't want to get rid of us."

She might love us. I mean, probably. She's our mom. But that doesn't mean she wants us here. She *left* us. Pretty incontrovertible evidence that she doesn't want us around.

But I don't say that to Aarav. For some reason, he's always been easier on her, even though he had less time with her than I did. But I'm glad that Aarav and I are getting along right now, and I don't want to do anything to mess that up. I never want him to look at me again the way he did last night.

So instead, I shrug, take a big bite of my waffles, and try to smile while chewing as the Duke and Duchess of Somewhere I Wasn't Paying Attention To come over to say farewell to me and Aarav.

Royal life.

Not as glamorous as people think.

CHAPTER FIFTEEN

Day ten. The big 1-0. Double digits. I stare at the count-down calendar I've made in my closet. Tonight, I'll draw the long diagonal across the last four hash marks, completing two full sets of five days. The longest I've ever been on land before.

The Royal Festival is over, which means my career as an ambassador has ended before it even began. I've spent the last couple days sleeping too late and eating breakfast in bed, then floating aimlessly in the pool with Finnian, the two of us either complaining about how we're stuck up here indefinitely for "safety reasons," or wondering when we are going to get in trouble for the Pirate Polo Match prank.

Still no punishment. Every time I've seen Mom recently, she's either so harried she ignores me completely, or she shoots me a weird, too-long stare, like she's waiting for me to explode or something. I can't believe Finnian and I got off with absolutely no consequences, but so far, zilch. And anytime I've tried to ask someone about what's going on with the duchy of Quimby, all I hear is that it's "a problem for next year."

Why should I even bother getting dressed? The Royal Festival is over, and I have nothing planned. Forget this. I'm going back to bed. I practically skip out of the closet and jump back into bed, pulling the thick duvet over my head and shutting out the world.

I must have fallen back asleep, because the next thing I know, someone is shaking my shoulder.

"Lana." It's Mom. "Lana, come on. You need to wake up. It's almost noon."

"Nnnnghhh."

I burrow deeper under the duvet, where she can't get to me.

"This is ridiculous," Mom says. *"This has gone on long enough. We need to get you kids back to Clarion already."*

"Ex*cuse* me?" I pop out of the blankets like a little eel wriggling out of the rocks. I knew she wanted to get rid of us, but to hear her actually say it hurts. "I can't believe you," I snap at her. "Can't you at least *pretend* you want us around?"

"You heard that?" Mom pales.

"Yes, I heard that!" I sigh with exasperation. "You just said it!"

"No, Lana. No, I didn't." Mom shakes her head. "I didn't say anything."

"Why are you lying?! I heard you, just now! You said, clearly, that you needed to get us back to Clarion."

"I didn't say anything, Lana. I swear. But I did . . . Well. I *thought* it."

"You *thought* it," I repeat. "You mean... I heard your thoughts? Nope. No way. That's not possible."

"Well..."

"Our powers don't work on land. Even the tiniest little mer-baby knows that."

"They do," Mom says. "You *can* read everyone else's minds. It simply takes a while for your powers to adjust on dry land. Ten days, to be exact. Which is why you've never stayed longer than seven days, just to be safe. But today is day ten, and..."

No. This can't be happening! I've spent the last seven years telling *everyone* that mer-telepathy doesn't work on land. I'd be less surprised if she'd just told me the sky wasn't blue.

"I never wanted Lana to have to deal with this," Mom says, only she's not saying it. Her lips aren't moving at all, but I can hear her thoughts as clearly as if she'd spoken them out loud. *"She must be so overwhelmed. And right now she's only listening to my thoughts. What happens when she leaves the room and has to hear everyone? It's going to be awful. But she can't stay trapped in here indefinitely, like a prisoner."*

I clap my hands over my ears, trying to block her out.

"Oh, poor Lana. Don't think about anything. Keep your mind totally blank, Hyacinth," Mom thinks. *"Especially don't think about kissing Petyr. Don't-think-about-kissing-Petyr-don't-think-about-kissing-Petyr."*

"MOM!" I scream. "That's not working!"

"What do I do how do I help her this was never supposed to happen remember when Lana was a baby and she would just sit in my

lap and look up at me with the sweetest, gummiest little smiles and her two tiny teeth she never looks at me like that anymore—"

"I have to get out of here," I say, desperate to escape the rising tide of Mom's frantic thoughts. They're coming faster and faster, overwhelming me. "I have to get out of here!"

As quickly as I can, I shove all the blankets off me and jump off the bed, my feet landing on the floor with a thud.

"It's okay, Lana," Mom says out loud. "Everything is going to be completely fine. Let's just take a deep breath, calm down, and hang out here, just the two of us, until you get used to this a little bit more." Her voice is calm, but it's competing with the cacophony inside her head. I can still hear Mom's random thoughts about me as a baby and worries about what's going to happen to me, and I do not need to hear any of it. I jam my fingers in my ears, but it doesn't help. Why is this happening? Under the sea, I only hear what people want me to hear. Not every passing thought!

"Aarav," Mom thinks clearly, the name cutting through her insane jumble of thoughts about my infancy and King Petyr and how she needs more coffee.

Aarav. She's right. I have to get to Aarav. He's probably freaking out!

Still in my pajamas, I race into the hall and slam the door shut behind me. I can still hear her, faintly, as I start running down the hall. But as I go, things only get worse. Now there are even more voices in my head. I hear someone from housekeeping wondering about the source of a stain on the carpet. Someone else worrying that she'll be late picking her kids up from school. Another person trying to decide what to have for lunch. Words, words, words bouncing around in my brain, filling it up with noise and chaos and other people's voices.

Finally, I've made it to Aarav's room.

"Aarav!" I shout, banging on his door. "Aarav! Are you there? It's me! Lana! Open up!"

Nothing. I press my ear to the door, but I can't hear any thoughts coming from inside. Well, like Mom said, it's almost noon. He's probably not still in bed.

I have to find him. I race toward the Royal Basketball Court, and as I hit the main floor of the palace, there are so many more people—castle staff and courtiers and who knows who else—that the sound is almost unbearable.

"Is she wearing pajamas?" I hear people thinking.

"Is that Princess Lana?"

"Why is Princess Lana wearing pajamas?"

"Mermaids must not understand what clothes are."

On and on and on. As I pass by the Royal Banquet Hall, there are enough people eating lunch that the roar of their thoughts becomes a static threatening to split my head in two. I grit my teeth and run past as quickly as I can, down the hall and, hopefully, toward Aarav.

As I make my way to the basketball court, thankfully, there are fewer people. All I hear is a member of the cleaning staff who must have a song stuck in their head, because it's the same tuneless refrain over and over. Finally, finally, I push open the heavy double doors of the gym, and see Aarav standing in the center of the court, alone. He dribbles a few times, then takes the shot. It swishes neatly through the net.

"Aarav!" I cry, squashing him into a hug. "Are you okay? How are you feeling?"

"I'm fine, Lana," he says, eyeing me suspiciously as he thinks, *"What is going on with her lately? Ever since we got here, life with Lana has had more ups and downs than typhoon season."*

"Hey!" I protest. "I'm not a typhoon. I'm doing the best I can."

Aarav's eyes widen. "I'm sorry—I mean—wait, what? How did you hear that?"

"Can't you hear me?" I think, but Aarav doesn't respond—either in his mind or with his words. He just stares back at me like I'm a few polyps short of a coral reef.

"Lana can hear my thoughts?" he thinks. *"That's not possible."*

"Yes, I can hear your thoughts!" I shout. "Apparently, it is possible! Can't you hear mine?"

"I don't . . . I don't think so?"

"Let's try." I grab his hands, like that might connect us more, somehow. *"Hi, Aarav,"* I think clearly. *"What did you have for breakfast?"*

Aarav stares at me blankly.

"Did you do it?" he asks.

"Yes." Now I'm starting to panic. Mom made it sound like this would happen to any merpeople who stayed on land for ten days. So why is it only me?

"Let's try again," Aarav suggests.

I take a deep breath, stare deep into his eyes like I can send the thoughts into his brain by willpower alone, and think, *"Basketball is confusing."*

That'll get a reaction.

But it doesn't.

"I'm sorry, Lana." Aarav drops my hands. "I don't hear anything."

"I don't understand," I whisper. "Why is this only happening to me?! Is there something wrong with me?"

"Nothing's wrong with you!" Aarav protests immediately. "We'll . . . We'll figure this out. Together. I promise."

He can't hear a thing. How is this possible?

While part of me is glad Aarav doesn't have to go through this, the other part of me can't believe I have to experience it all by myself.

I'm in this alone.

CHAPTER SIXTEEN

After leaving Aarav, I spent all of yesterday in my room, too overwhelmed by all the thoughts I could hear. Mom must have told everybody I was sick or something, because nobody bothered me. Finnian didn't even stop by to see if I wanted to go to the Natatorium.

Finnian. I wish he was in on this with me. Then we could talk, just the two of us, with nobody listening in, like we do at home.

It's kind of boring in my quarters, but at least when I'm on the balcony, all I can hear are the waves and the seagulls. I lean on the railing, close my eyes, and let the wind whip my hair around.

"Probably should have knocked," I hear Mom think.

"Mom!" I jump. "Don't startle a person on a balcony! That feels obvious!"

"Sorry," she says sheepishly. "So what's the plan for today?" She leans against the balcony next to me, looking out at the waves. She's doing a much better job of controlling her thoughts now. "Gonna hide out up here and watch the seagulls?"

"I named that one Herbert." I point to the seagull flying past us at the moment. "His wife should be along any minute. Her name is Hortense."

"While chronicling the life and times of the seagulls *does* sound like a ton of fun . . . I think it's time for you to leave your room."

I hesitate for a moment, trying to decide how much to share with her. Well, there's no point in hiding my feelings. It's all out there now.

"It's impossible." I shake my head. "There are too many people, thinking too many things. I can't handle it."

"There's a lot of places you could go where there wouldn't be a lot of people. Down to the gardens. Out to the beach. Into the stables. I'm sure the horses are only thinking about hay." Mom whinnies and then says, "Good oats!" in what I think is supposed to be a horse voice.

"I can't hear animal thoughts, Mom." I laugh at her ridiculous impression.

I don't remember her being goofy like this.

"Probably for the best. The seagulls are intrusive enough already."

"So . . . why is this happening to me? I mean, why is this happening to *just* me?" When I haven't been stalking seagulls, my thoughts keep returning to this one question. "Why can't Aarav hear my thoughts?"

"I don't really know." Mom shakes her head. I can hear her thinking how badly she wishes she had a better answer for me. "We're kind of in uncharted waters. There have been very, very

few half human, half merpeople over the centuries. Everything I've read in the castle library said your powers would activate on your tenth day on land, but all those records were about adults, and there weren't enough of them to provide conclusive data." I consider this. It's weird knowing there have been so few people like me in history. "Maybe Aarav's too young," she continues. "Maybe his human side is stronger than his mer side. But these are all just theories."

"I guess that makes sense. Honestly, I'm just glad he doesn't have to deal with this."

"I'm sorry that you have to. But it's time to go outside, Lana," Mom says. "You can't just hide away in here because it's hard." Sort of harsh, but her voice is kind. "Face the world. Like a true Princess of Clarion."

"Fine."

Anything for Clarion. And I *was* getting kind of bored in here anyway. Plus, that idea about going to the stables isn't half-bad. Maybe this is the year I finally get on a horse! I guess I have nothing else to do, now that our visit has been extended indefinitely.

Mom waits while I step into my closet to dress, like she's worried I'm going to change my mind and hop right back into bed the second she steps out of the room. I pull on a dress quickly, then settle my abalone around my neck as I walk toward her.

"That necklace," Mom thinks as she looks at me. *"Oh, Lana."* Her face falls. "That isn't a necklace at all, is it?" she says out loud. "That's the ambassador's abalone of Clarion. I can't believe I didn't recognize it right away."

"Oh. Um, yeah." I fiddle with the chain. "Dad made me an ambassador right before I left."

"That's why she wanted a schedule. I cannot believe Carrack didn't tell me about this," she thinks angrily. *"No, I can't believe I didn't notice. I've been too busy with Petyr, and the treaty, and—"*

"It's okay, Mom," I cut her off, trying to stop the rising tide of her thoughts. I can't believe I'm reassuring her about this, after being upset that she hasn't noticed for so long, but I can hear in her thoughts how badly she really feels about it. Listening to her beat herself up isn't nearly as satisfying as you'd expect.

"I'm sorry, Lana." She stands up and gives me a hug. I let her hug me, but I stand there stiffly, unable to fully relax into it. "An ambassador! I'm so proud of you. Your dad must be, too."

"Yeah." I take a step back awkwardly. It's nice to hear that she's proud of me, but it doesn't change the fact that my first Royal Festival as an ambassador was a big fail. "I mean, not that it's meant much. I thought I'd get to do more, and I probably should have tried harder, but . . . well. It's still cool."

"Maybe next year?" Mom squeezes my shoulder. "Now let's go. You can head outside, and I've got to join the treaty negotiations with Fremont."

"That's still happening? I thought all the political stuff ended when the Royal Festival did."

"It was supposed to, but . . . it's proved unexpectedly complicated."

"That's great! Well, it's not great that it's complicated," I

amend, "but I can come with you! See how treaties are actually made! It's not too late for me to be an ambassador this year!"

"Oh, I don't think you'd be interested in any of this!" Mom says jovially, but I can see her fidgeting nervously with the sleeves of her gown. "It's mostly footnotes. We'll find something much better for you to be involved with next year."

"But I'm interested in footnotes." Why is she fighting me on this? Just for a second, I believed she really wanted to spend time with me! "That's where a lot of the important stuff gets done. Dad always says diplomacy is in the details."

"Your father is . . . not wrong," she says carefully. I can almost feel her trying to control her thoughts. "But I don't think it's a good idea."

"I won't even say anything. I can just sit there and listen. I could learn so much."

"I just don't think it's a good idea *right now*," Mom emphasizes. "This is a delicate treaty, and you're trying to navigate this new power, and that makes you . . . well . . ."

"A liability," I finish for her. She didn't want to say it, but I heard her think it before she could stop herself.

"Next year, Lana. I promise."

"Forget it." I brush past her into the hallway.

"Lana—"

"I said *forget it*!"

A liability? I am *not* a liability. If Mom knew me at all, she'd know how seriously I take government. And if she stopped to think for a moment, she might realize that it might actually

be *useful* to have someone in the room who could *read minds* during a complicated treaty negotiation?!

I burst through the doors behind the palace and step onto the giant stone patio where Grandma sometimes hosts summer parties or Royal Garden Club meetings. Down a set of stairs, her rose garden encircles a giant fountain, and then rolling green lawns beyond. When we first got here, each rose was absolutely perfect. Now they're losing their petals and turning brown at the edges, starting to wilt.

It's kind of how I feel.

I take a seat at the edge of the fountain, listening to the splashing and running my hand through the water, taking a little comfort at a small piece of home. Then I hear static, the buzzing growing louder. Oh no. Thoughts. And it's the absolute *worst* thoughts. Lady Daffodil and Lady Carnation are coming toward me, their thoughts so fast and furious that they're entering my mind in a jumble. Above the static, I can pick out "*hair,*" "*fountain,*" and I think "*avocado,*" but that's it.

"Do you smell something?" Lady Daffodil crinkles her nose as she stops in front of me at the fountain. "Smells kind of like the beach."

"Like sunscreen and coconuts?" Lady Carnation says. She thinks, *"I love the beach. I love summer. Sum-sum-summertime. Swimming. Ice cream. Mmm, ice cream. Is it too early for ice cream?"*

"No!" Daffodil snaps. "Like . . . seaweed! And old fish!" Daffodil laughs meanly, her pert nose crinkling.

"Why are you even still here?" I ask.

"We live in the Hills." Daffodil tosses her head arrogantly. Oh, right. I keep forgetting. "I suppose you're not familiar with the truly important people here."

"Obviously she doesn't remember that we live in the Hills. Why would she know anything about me?" Daffodil thinks. *"I'm not anyone important. Not like Lana."*

My mouth falls open.

"What are you staring at, freak?" Daffodil says, challenging me. And then she thinks, *"Lana thinks I'm a loser. I knew it. Look at the way she's staring at me! Is there something wrong with my face? There must be something wrong with my face."*

Daffodil rubs her hand along her jawline, trying to be casual.

"Not staring!" I quickly look away, surprised to find myself feeling bad for Daffodil.

"Um. Okay. Whatever. Weirdo."

"Great," Daffodil thinks as she walks away, tugging Lady Carnation behind her. *"Lana obviously thinks I'm such a freak. Because I am."*

She keeps beating herself up until she's far enough away that her thoughts fade into static. I almost want to run after her and tell her that she's not a freak, but then I remember the way she treated Aarav.

Still. Daffodil cares what I think about her? That makes absolutely no sense. Why has she been such a jerk the whole time I've been up here?!

I leave the fountain, heading in the opposite direction from

Lady Daffodil in hopes of being alone with my thoughts. As I head along the back of the palace, I pass a guard standing at attention.

"What a brat," he thinks as I walk by him, his face impassive. *"Entitled Princess Lana, waltzing all around like she owns the place."*

He thinks I'm a brat?! But he doesn't even know me! What could I possibly have done to annoy a literal stranger? This guard I don't know thinks I stink, but Lady Daffodil thinks I'm too cool for her?

Maybe I should have ignored Mom and stayed in bed all day. The world is way too confusing when you know what people actually think of you.

Around this side of the palace, there's a little gazebo surrounded by rosebushes where Grandma sometimes takes tea in the afternoon. Grandma's there right now, and instead of her crown, there's a large straw sun hat on her head. She's crouched down, pruning the rosebushes, a floral apron covering her dress. At her side, also wielding a pair of gardening shears, is Aarav. Hearing me approach, they stop fussing with the flowers. Aarav hops to his feet, then helps Grandma up. He pulls a handkerchief out of his pants pocket and mops the sweat off his brow.

"Hi, sweetheart," Grandma says.

"My beautiful Lana," she thinks as I join them. *"I wish we could spend more time together. One of these days I need to get over my fear of breathing underwater and go visit my grandbabies. I'm sure*

the magical gills the Royal Sorcerer conjures are perfectly safe; it's just the thought of all that water above my head. . . . "

I smile at her guiltily. I had no idea Grandma was scared to come visit us below the waves. I scratch at the back of my neck, unsure if I'm uncomfortable because of the unexpected warmth of the sun or because of what I just heard. I should have been making more of an effort to spend time with her up here, not just this year, but at every Royal Festival. The thought of all the time I've wasted up here sulking, when I could have been spending it with Grandma and Grandpa, unsettles my stomach. I even bailed on Grandma for the Teddy Bear Tea Party. I'm the worst.

"Hi, Lana!" Aarav says, his smile open and encouraging. "Do you want to garden with us?"

"How about you two finish up here, and I'll check in on the Empress Josephine roses." Grandma pats Aarav's shoulder. "Fussy little things. But they'll learn to bloom where they're planted."

Grandma winks at us, waves off Aarav's offer of help, and walks toward the back of the garden, her back straight. Even in an apron and a sun hat, there's no mistaking the fact that she's a queen.

"Poor Lana," Aarav thinks. Since I'm still watching Grandma go, he must not have taken the time to pull his thoughts together and filter out what I can hear. *"I feel so sorry for her. She'll never know how much fun it is to get sweaty, dig around in the dirt, and watch things grow. She'll never enjoy all that life on land has to offer."*

"You feel *sorry* for me?!" I ask. Aarav meets my eyes, guilt painted all over his face. "You don't need to feel sorry for me, okay?" I say quietly. "I'm fine. I'm totally fine."

"You really don't seem fine."

I start to protest, then stop myself. He's right. I'm not fine. I'm a *liability*, apparently.

"Wanna help?" Aarav hands me a little shovel. I can hear him thinking about how badly he wants me to join him, how badly he wants me to understand some of the reasons he likes it up here.

Wordlessly, I take the little shovel and start to dig where Aarav points.

I've had enough of words for today.

CHAPTER SEVENTEEN

"I am so *jealous*!" Finnian says as we reach the shed at the outer edges of the Royal Gardens. "When your mom said nobody could see you, I thought it was because you had sea lice or something."

"Gross!" I object. "I don't have sea lice! I have *never* had sea lice!"

"But then Aarav told me you have *magic powers*."

After we finished gardening, I went up to my room to change into something a little less dirt-splattered. Aarav must have run into Finnian without me, because by the time I finished changing, my best friend was waiting outside my door with his cloak and a huge grin.

"I don't have magic powers," I scoff. "It's the same thing everybody can do back home."

"Yeah. But *nobody* can do it here." Finnian's eyes are glowing. "Which makes it basically magic."

We're at the very outer edges of the Royal Gardens, hiding

behind a little firewood shed that no one should come anywhere near until winter hits. I rest my back against the shed, feeling at ease for the first time since I started hearing everyone's thoughts.

"I just don't understand why *I* can't read everyone's minds," Finnian muses.

"Well, theoretically, your powers should kick in on your tenth day on land, but Aarav's didn't. So they might not. "

"Oh, I'm sure it'll happen for me." He rubs his hands together eagerly. "Can't wait."

"What I don't understand is why I can't read *your* mind," I say. I stare into Finnian's eyes, and he stares back. Just like when I first ran into him, all I hear is a pleasant hum. It's nice not to be bombarded by Finnian's thoughts, but the fact that it's different from everyone else is kind of freaking me out. "It's so weird."

"It's not that weird. I've always been extraordinary," Finnian says. "You probably can't read my thoughts because my mind is so complex."

"Or it's because your skull is so thick." I reach up to knock on top of his head.

"Gentle with the genius's head, please." He swats me away. "Now let's focus on the important stuff. The *interesting* stuff."

"Like what?"

"Like the fact that you need to find the *fun* in your new power."

"Nothing about this is *fun*." Seriously? He is unbelievable.

"Finding out people hate me isn't fun. Having hundreds of voices blasting into my head isn't *fun*."

"You're doing it wrong, Lana," Finnian says kindly. "We have to *find* the fun. Come on." He stands up and extends his hand. "Let's go. It's time to shake things up."

"Go where?" I ask suspiciously. "The last time we tried to 'shake things up,' it didn't work out so well for either of us."

"Even I can admit that may have been a minor miscalculation." This is the closest I'll ever get to remorse from Finnian. "But this time? No bubbles, no pranks, no stampeding royalty. Promise." He holds up his hands innocently. "Just a simple little field trip. Let's go out."

"Out?" I repeat. "We are out."

"No, we're *outside*," he corrects me. "Let's go out. Like leave the castle grounds."

The castle grounds? I have *never* gone beyond the walls. Not once. Not ever. Not even for a minute during any of the Royal Festivals I've been to.

Of course, I've never been stuck in the castle for this long before, either.

"I don't know if that's such a good idea," I say warily.

I *say* it's not such a good idea, but I follow him anyway. The idea of seeing something new is pretty appealing. And at least I know I'm not the only one who's susceptible to Finnian's charisma. When he was visiting Clarion last year, he almost got elected to the senate after convincing enough people to write him in on the ballot.

(Obviously, Finnian did not become a senator of Clarion, as he is a teenager and doesn't even live there.)

Not far from where we've been sitting behind the woodshed, the fields end at a stone wall covered in ivy that encircles the entire perimeter of the castle. The grounds are so vast, it's easy to forget that we're actually kind of trapped in here.

Having reached the wall, Finnian starts tapping against it like he's looking for something, lifting and pulling leaves out of the way. Eventually, he grabs a big chunk of ivy and pulls it to the side, exposing a small wooden door in the stone.

"How did you even know this was here?" I ask, stunned.

"You never know when you might need an escape route," he says, which is probably the most Finnian thing he could possibly say.

He pushes the door, and it swings open easily. Once we're on the other side, Finnian shuts it and pats the ivy on the outer wall into place. If you didn't know there was a door here, you'd never be able to spot it.

On this side of the wall, there's nothing but a long dirt road, more fields on the other side of it, and clear blue sky. Decisively, Finnian turns right and starts walking, like he knows exactly where he's going.

As I follow Finnian down the dirt road, with nothing in my head but my own thoughts and the gentle hum from Finnian, I feel lighter than I have since I first gained this awful new power. More quickly than I would have thought possible, my nervousness at leaving the palace has been replaced by a sense of, well, something like freedom.

There's a chill in the air that definitely wasn't here this morning—it's a good thing I grabbed a cloak when I left my room. I guess fall is coming. Although I've heard people talk about it, I've never been topside long enough to see that leaves turn into different colors. It sounds like nothing we have at home. The idea that I might be stuck here as the seasons change—far longer than just the week of the Royal Festival, like usual—should depress me beyond belief. But right now, feeling the cool breeze and looking up at the blue sky, Finnian at my side, I can almost understand what Aarav finds so appealing about life up here.

Almost.

In just a few minutes of walking, the dirt road changes to cobblestones. Finnian has led us right into downtown Hobben's Hill, the capital city of the kingdom of the Hills. The buildings here are taller than anything we have under the sea; they almost look like three or four wooden houses squashed on top of each other, with pointy thatched roofs on the tops. All around us, people are talking and thinking, and the noise should feel like a horrible jumble in my mind. But instead, all the different voices meld together in a messy way that somehow works, almost like a song.

"You okay?" Finnian asks, checking in on me. "It's not too much? Up here?" He taps his head.

"Not too much."

A man passes us, trying to remember his grocery list. *"Eggs, flour, sugar, milk,"* he thinks, over and over again. *"Eggs, flour, sugar, milk."* I almost laugh. His face is so serious, you'd think he was thinking about something far more important than groceries.

We arrive in a cobblestone square that must be the center of Hobben's Hill. There's a fountain right in the middle with children running along the edge, dipping their toes in the water. I can hear a chorus of different mothers thinking *"Don't fall!"* while all the children think about is splashing. Although people probably live in the upper floors of the buildings, the ground floors are all shops and restaurants. And lots of them have little stalls in the open air, selling things like bread and jam and ice cream.

A woman walks by me, rubbing her arms. *"Chilly,"* she thinks. *"I should have brought my cloak. There's no way I can go home to get it before work."*

"Wait!" The woman stops and looks at me, confused. "Here you go." I unfasten the clasp of my cloak and hand it to her. Suddenly, I'm warm all over. "Take it."

"Um . . . are you sure?" She still looks confused, but I can hear her thinking about what a nice cloak it is.

"Totally sure." She takes it, smiling, and I smile back. "Have a nice day!" I call as she hurries off, still thinking about being late for work but feeling happier as she pulls on the cloak and warms up. "She was cold," I explain to Finnian when he looks at me quizzically.

"And there's no way you could have known that without your powers. See? They're good!" he says triumphantly. "They let you do that 'Do-Gooder Lana, the People's Princess' thing you love so much."

I punch him in the arm, but I can't stop smiling. I *do* like helping people. I think it's one of the best things about being a princess.

We wander past the different stalls, and I hear the vendors thinking about how much they hope they'll sell today, and all the shoppers calculating what they can afford. We stop in front of the ice cream stall, drawn inexorably toward the beautiful tubs in a rainbow of colors. There's a man and an adorable little girl standing in front of us, right next to the case.

"Can we get ice cweam, Daddy?" she asks, tugging on his arm.

"I wish we could," the man thinks, *"but I can't afford it."*

Before he opens his mouth to tell her that she can't have any, I step in.

"Did you know," I say, bending down until I'm closer to the little girl's height, "that today is a very special day? It's actually Free Ice Cream Day in the Hills!"

"Fwee Ice Cweam Day?" she asks. She looks more excited than Aarav did on the birthday he got a sea pony.

"Free Ice Cream Day?! I've never heard of Free Ice Cream Day!" the ice cream man thinks, panicking. *"This is going to bankrupt me!"*

I reach out into the pocket of my dress—where Mom makes me carry money with me "in case of emergencies," even though I've never left the castle before and can't imagine what kind of emergency I could possibly get into while I'm inside that I'd have to buy my way out of—and pull out what I hope is more than enough money to buy ice cream for the man and his daughter. And Finnian and me, too, of course.

All this mind reading can really make you work up an appetite.

"Thank goodness," the ice cream man thinks, while the little girl's mind is just a chorus of "*Ice cream! Ice cream! Ice cream!*" And I don't even need to read the father's thoughts to see how happy he is.

As I watch the man and his daughter walk away, holding hands and eating their ice cream cones, I realize that *I'm* happy, too. Really happy. It could just be the strawberry ice cream, but it could be the fact that I'm starting to agree with Finnian— these powers might actually be good for something.

Also, ice cream is pretty awesome, even if it is a land thing. Dessert is the one place the ocean can't really compare.

"You know what?" I burst out laughing at Finnian's chocolate ice cream mustache. "What?" he says. "What, Lana? What?"

Eventually, I stop giggling enough to communicate that he has chocolate all over his face. He cleans himself up with a napkin.

"As I was saying, before you so viciously mocked me," he continues, pretending to glare at me, "I think it's time to take your powers to a professional level."

"Excuse me? Finnian, what—"

But before I can get Finnian to tell me what he means, he's already jumped on top of the fountain, perching on the edge where the little kids were playing when we first got here.

"Ladies and gentlemen, boys and girls!" he booms. "Step right up! Step right up and see the Amazing Lana!"

"Finnian," I hiss, tugging on the side of his pants, "what in the seven seas are you doing?"

"She will delight you. She will astound you. She will amaze you with her mystical powers!"

And because it's Finnian, and he can do this kind of thing, a fairly sizable crowd forms around him.

"You, sir!" Finnian points at a kid around our age, standing in the front and wearing a red shirt. "Think of a number! Any number!"

"Six," the kid thinks.

"Six," I blurt out automatically.

The kid looks surprised, but nods his head.

"I've got one!" A woman in the back raises her hand.

"Eighty-four!" I say, reading her mind. She claps, delighted that I got it right.

"I've got one," an older man says from the middle of the crowd.

"Four thousand, three hundred, twenty-eight. And eighteen cents?" I read his mind, confused as to why it threw cents in at the end there.

"Holy bovines," the man marvels. "There's no way she could have possibly known that!"

The crowd claps. This is fun! "Ma'am?" I say suddenly, struck by the thoughts of a woman in a green cloak. "Your neighbor isn't stealing from your garden. That was a deer. In fact, your neighbor *stopped* the deer from eating even more!"

Just like the rogue manatee and the kelp beds in Clarion!

"And, sir?" I point to a startled man in a blue scarf. "The woman standing next to you? Your friend? She thinks you have very fine eyes."

The two of them blush, smiling happily at each other. I go through the crowd, clearing up misunderstandings and sharing other nice thoughts. Finnian was right. This mind-reading thing might not be so bad.

CHAPTER EIGHTEEN

"Good morning!" The following morning, I open my bedroom door to see Finnian standing outside, munching on a waffle. "Want one?" He holds another one, wrapped in a linen napkin, out for me.

"Thanks." I take it and shut my door behind me, munching happily as we head down the hall. "Although I don't suppose you have any maple syrup tucked away inside that jacket?"

"Tomorrow," he promises. "I'll figure something out for tomorrow."

Knowing Finnian, he probably will.

Walking through the castle with Finnian by my side is so much better. The pleasant, gentle hum of his mind helps mute the noise of a crowd or the rush of words into my brain. At the top of the grand staircase, I see Aarav crossing the Grand Hall, dressed in his basketball clothes. I wave at him, and he stops, waiting for us to join him.

"I feel so left out," Aarav thinks as we descend the stairs,

surprising me. *"For the first time ever, Lana is going through something I can't understand. And Finnian, of all people, seems to know how to share it with her way better than I can."*

"Hi, Lana! Hey, Finnian," he says as we meet him in the hall, while thinking, very deliberately, *"Hi, Lana. Hey, Finnian."*

That's the thing about thoughts—even when you're trying to control them, whatever you *really* think has a way of slipping out first.

I never imagined that my powers activating like this would make Aarav feel left out. I wish he didn't. I don't *want* Aarav to have to understand! If anything, I'm *happy* for him—even though Finnian helped me see that there's a positive side to this, too, I still wouldn't want anyone to have to hear what everyone secretly thinks of them. Certainly not my little brother. (Although, because it's Aarav, I'm sure people only think nice things about him.)

Except, of course, for a select few losers, who also happen to be entering the Grand Hall at this exact moment. It's Lady Daffodil, Lady Carnation, and, the ultimate worst, the Crown Prince of Caversham. What is he even doing here? I *know* he doesn't live in the Hills. Argh!

"Oh, look!" The Crown Prince points at Aarav. "It's the little merboy!"

I grit my teeth as the three of them get closer, the menacing volume of the Crown Prince's thoughts blocking out whatever Daffodil and Carnation are thinking.

If only Daffodil would actually say what she's thinking. Now that I know she doesn't think all merpeople are uncool, I wish she'd stop acting like it. I'm trying to sympathize with her, but it's hard when she's treated my brother so badly.

"So do you still have a swim bladder in there?" The Crown Prince pokes Aarav in the tummy, like he can ferret out the answer by touch alone.

"Um, I don't—" Aarav stutters. "I mean, I'm not sure—"

"What's a swim bladder?" Daffodil asks. "It sounds gross."

"Fish use them to control their buoyancy," Carnation explains. "It's an internal gas-filled organ."

"Gas-filled organ." The Crown Prince giggles. "So you're full of farts?"

"Everyone's full of farts," Carnation points out.

The Crown Prince of Caversham makes an over-the-top fake fart noise.

What is he, six years old?

"Ew, Aarav, disgusting!" He waves his hand in front of his nose dramatically. "You smell even worse than usual."

Okay, that's *it*. I'm performing a citizen's arrest and sending him straight to the dungeons. If Grandpa needs to court-martial me, I'll deal with the consequences later.

But before I can step in, something amazing happens.

"I'd rather smell like a farting geoduck than share an IQ with one," Aarav says, clearly and confidently. "They don't have brains. A phenomenon that, unfortunately, you're very familiar with."

For all his bravado, Aarav is freaking out on the inside. *"Holy mackerel,"* he thinks. *"I can't believe I just said that."* But you'd never know what he was thinking from how cool and collected he looks. He stares down the Crown Prince of Caversham like Aarav is as big as a blue whale and Caversham is tiny and insignificant as a krill, even though the other prince towers over him.

The Crown Prince sneers, but I'm sure I'm not the only one who sees his lip wobble. He turns and leaves the Grand Hall quickly, without even attempting to think of a comeback. Aarav crushed him completely.

"Perfect," Lady Daffodil thinks. *"Now Lana must think I'm even more of a loser than she did already!"*

She scurries after the Crown Prince of Caversham, Lady Carnation following in her shadow like always. You know what? I wouldn't think Daffodil was a loser if she'd stop following this creep of a prince around, or tried to keep him from tormenting my brother. I keep finding myself torn between feeling bad for her and angry that she doesn't have the courage to say what she's really thinking.

Well, one thing isn't confusing at all. I am so proud of Aarav. I look at him as he watches his bullies scuttle away, his head held high.

"I'm gonna go play basketball with Von," Aarav says.

"Do you think you can handle more dunking? I thought you might be tired from dunking so hard on the Crown Prince of Caversham," I tease.

Aarav laughs. "Why is he still here? I thought all the visiting royalty left."

"Some of the royalty stayed behind because they didn't accomplish everything they wanted to. Fremont is still working on the Peace and Friendship Treaty." Right. Without me. Because I'm a *liability.* "And the Royal Family of Caversham is still here because they're trying to convince Mom to lift the trade sanctions on imports from the glass slipper factory in Caversham. But there's no way that's going to happen. We all know Mom's feelings on glass slippers."

"Not enough arch support," Aarav and I chorus, laughing.

"Gotta go," Aarav says. "Von's waiting for me. See you guys later."

I wave as Aarav heads toward the basketball court, his thoughts a happy jumble of basketball and Von and his pride in making strides with those bullies. It's so nice to see Aarav branching out on his own. And of course I love spending time with him, but right now? Now I have to worry about Aarav feeling sorry for me, not to mention left out, and trying to control what he thinks around me all the time. Hanging out with Finnian is a *lot* less complicated.

Everything would be so much easier if we could just go home. There, my powers would be totally normal, instead of complicating everything. I'd be just like everyone else.

Maybe it's time to try messaging Dad again....They must have made *some* progress on rebuilding Clarion by now.

"Where should we go today?" Finnian asks. "Take our show on the road? See how many citizens of the Hills we can delight with the amazing talents of the mystical Lana and her magic mind reading?"

"Nah." I shrug. I'm feeling great, and although reading people's minds was fun yesterday, today I kind of want to relax.

I start to think about places that make me feel relaxed—the Natatorium, the beach, really any body of water—and then I realize it might be fun to do something totally and completely different.

"Hey, Finnian," I ask, "have you ever been on a horse?"

CHAPTER NINETEEN

The Royal Stables in the Hills are made entirely of white-painted wood with golden accents—which seems to me like a poor decorating choice for the home of some of the messiest land animals I've encountered, but what do I know? I'm no horse expert. Finnian and I walk through the huge open doors of the stable, looking around at the different horse noses poking out over various pens.

"Uh-oh," Finnian says. I turned around to look through the barn doors. "Isn't that your mom?" He points over the hill, where, sure enough, Mom and King Petyr are thundering toward us and the Royal Stables on matching white horses.

Finnian points to a bush in the distance. "I'm just gonna go . . . hide . . . over there." He takes off running.

"Why are you hiding?" I shout after him.

"Because she's probably still mad about the bubbles thing!" he calls as he sprints away.

"She's mad at me, too!"

"She's your *mom*! She has to forgive you!" I'm not so sure

about that—especially after our fight. I watch Finnian dive headfirst into a bush. Some help *he* is. I hope there's something slightly itchy in that bush. Not debilitatingly poisonous, just mildly annoying.

Because that's how I feel right now. Mildly annoyed.

"Lana!" Mom says with surprise as she and King Petyr dismount their horses, handing the reins to a groom before walking to meet me in the stable. Mom might be saying something, but if she is, I miss it entirely—because King Petyr is thinking something that captures *all* of my attention.

"These horses will be perfect for pulling the wedding carriage," King Petyr thinks. *"Two white horses, a white-and-gold carriage, Hyacinth looking beautiful in her white dress . . . I can't wait for the wedding. How did I get so lucky? I can't believe I get to marry Hyacinth."*

What. Is. Happening.

"*Marry* her?!" I shriek, like King Petyr just proposed barbecuing my mother. "Nobody said *anything* about a wedding."

"Lana," Mom says placatingly.

"Are you guys getting married?" I ask, confronting her.

"We are," Mom confirms, reaching out for Petyr's hand like she needs his support.

I'm gutted, and the worst part is, I don't even know *why* I'm crushed. It's not like I ever thought my mom would come home. Or like I thought that we'd be a family again.

. . . Right?

"I just don't understand why you didn't tell me," I say stiffly, summoning every ounce of my princess politeness to keep my true feelings from bubbling up to the surface. I'm starting to feel out of control again, in that way I *hate*, and I don't want Mom or King Petyr to see me as anything less than together.

Thank goodness she can't read *my* thoughts.

"We couldn't," Mom says in a rush. "We couldn't tell anyone. I wanted to tell you right away, of course I did, and I really wanted you here this year because we'd hoped to have the wedding at the end of the Royal Festival, but it's all proved unexpectedly complicated, and no one outside of the negotiation room could know...."

As Mom talks, my mind is spinning. I had just gotten used to the fact that my mom has a boyfriend, and now she's about to have a husband? A royal husband, with his own kingdom and—

His own kingdom.

Of *course*.

Understanding finally crashes over me, like waves breaking against a rocky coastline.

"The treaty," I say. Mom and King Petyr look confused. "That's why you couldn't tell anyone about the wedding. And this is why the Hills-Fremont treaty's been so difficult to negotiate. It's not just about Peace and Friendship. It's about borders."

"Well, in a way, yes—" Mom starts.

"No wonder the other land countries are nervous!" Everything finally makes sense. "What happens when the two of you get married? Will you live in Fremont? And what happens when Mom inherits the throne of the Hills? Do the Hills and Fremont become one superpower nation?"

"The treaty outlines a plan for unity with autonomy, effective upon Hyacinth's coronation," King Petyr says. "There's precedent for something like this."

"Precedent? You mean like during Mom's first royal marriage? To Dad?"

Remember him? The apparently not-so-happy union that resulted in my existence? What's *he* going to think about this?

"Yes," Mom says briskly, but her cheeks color. "One set of monarchs, two parliaments to ensure that all citizens feel their interests are being represented. We're finally making some progress on the treaty, and I think we're about to come to a conclusion that satisfies everyone. We should have it ratified and be standing at the altar within the week."

"Within the *week*?" Sweet Poseidon. I am so not ready for this. Call over one of the Royal Stable Hands; they'll have to take a break from scooping poop to shovel my jaw off the floor. "Does anyone know about this except for the diplomats at the Royal Festival? What about the citizens of Fremont and the Hills? What will they think? And will the other countries even *let* you get married, or will they see this wedding as an act of aggression? Does Caversham invade once the cake is cut?"

"Lana," Mom says. "Once the other countries see the finished treaty, I'm confident that they'll understand that nothing is amiss. Ever since he announced the treaty at the Welcome Ball, Grandpa has had the Hills' finest political minds smoothing the way with our neighboring nations. We wanted to keep the wedding under wraps until we knew the exact terms of the finished treaty, but everything will be fine. This isn't something you have to worry about."

"Yes, it *is*!" I am so sick and tired of adults telling me not to worry about things that actually affect me—and Clarion. "Although you keep conveniently forgetting the fact, I am an ambassador. And it is literally my *job* to worry about how the potential merger of two powerful countries affects other nations, including my own. Everything flows out to sea eventually."

"Lana, let's all sit down for a minute and talk about this," Mom says.

"No thanks."

I need to process. Or at least attempt to process. Mom is getting *married*, and I'm personally overwhelmed by that news. But like everything else about being royal, it's not just personal. It's political. Maybe I'm focusing too *much* on the political, but that feels safer than trying to unpack how I feel about Mom getting remarried.

Constitutional law I understand.

My feelings about Mom? Not so much.

I need a minute to breathe, away from Mom and King Petyr.

"Lana, please, wait—"

I leave the stable, ignoring Mom's calls. I'm not ready to talk about this at all, and especially not with her.

As I pass by the bush Finnian is hiding in, he pops his head out of the shrubbery. "What did I miss?" he asks, bewildered. I don't stick around long enough to answer him.

CHAPTER TWENTY

I ran to the safest place I could think of: the beach. As close as possible to home without actually being there. I wish I could stick my toes in the water, just for a minute, but as soon as I touched the salt water, I'd be back to having a tail. And don't get me wrong, that sounds amazing, but the idea of someone accidentally stumbling across me while I'm flip-flopping between fins and feet is just too awkward for words.

Down the beach, nestled in a little rocky outcropping along the shore, there's a small cave that nobody ever visits. I haven't been in there since three Royal Festivals ago, when I dropped a plate on the toes of the Prime Minister of Framden and it shattered, making a big noise and a huge mess. At the time, I'd thought that was the most embarrassed and upset I could ever be at a Royal Festival.

Now that whole situation feels laughable.

Mom is getting *married*. I knew she wasn't coming back—I *knew* that—but somehow, it feels like she left me all over again. And worst of all, she didn't even tell me. I guess I understand why she had to keep the wedding secret from some of the other countries until they finalized the treaty, but that didn't mean she had to keep it a secret from *me*. I wouldn't have told anyone! When you're royalty, there's the country and then there's your family, but I always thought family was stronger. The most important thing.

Now? I don't know what to think.

I'm not sure how long I stay there, but just when I'm starting to think there might be such a thing as too much alone time, I hear a gentle humming. It grows louder, and louder, and in just a few minutes, Finnian pops his head into the cave.

"I didn't think anybody else knew about this place. How did you even know I was here?" I ask as he walks toward me, hopping over puddles and carefully stepping on stones.

"Because I'm always in tune with you, Lana," he says, so sincerely I know he has to be joking. Sincere is not a mode that Finnian operates in. He sits on the rock beside me. "Well, I went to the beach, because I thought you'd want to be close to home. And when I didn't see you, I thought I'd try the cave. This cave is actually an escape route from the castle," he says. "Leads right from a storage basement into a tunnel and out to the sea. Always know your exits." He taps his nose wisely.

I roll my eyes good-naturedly. He's ridiculous, but I'm glad to see him. Finnian may know all the exits, but I'm the one who needs to escape.

"What happened?" he asks, more gently than I'm used to from him.

"Mom and Petyr didn't tell you?"

"Nope." He shakes his head. "I popped into the stable to see what was going on, but they were having kind of a heated discussion. So I just did an awkward bow and left."

I snort, imagining the normally smooth Finnian fleeing the stable, scared of Mom.

"So what happened?" he asks again, still gentle, but pressing me.

"She's getting *married*." Saying it out loud makes it feel more real, but it's still hard to believe. "Mom. My mother. Is getting *married*. To King Petyr."

"Whoa." Finnian looks as surprised as I felt. "And you had no idea?"

"Nope."

"She didn't tell you—"

"Nope."

"And when are they—"

"As soon as possible. Probably within the week."

"This *week*?!" Finnian's voice rises at the end, high-pitched like a dolphin. "Wow. Okay. Whoa. Yeah, no. That's not gonna happen."

"It's definitely happening. King Petyr's even picked out his perfect wedding ponies," I add glumly.

"Not if we have anything to say about it. We have to do something to break up the happy couple."

"Don't be ridiculous."

"*I'm* not ridiculous. This situation is ridiculous! Come on, Lana! *A week?!* And she didn't tell you?!"

I pause, unsure of what to say. I probably shouldn't even have told Finnian that Mom and Petyr are getting married, but I *definitely* shouldn't get into everything with the treaty. Regardless of how I'm feeling, this wedding has all kinds of political ramifications that Finnian doesn't know about. Mom said they'd just about finished up the negotiations. If we break her and Petyr up now, that could mess with everything. And King Petyr seems mild-mannered, but who knows what would happen if Mom dumped him. Would Fremont retaliate? Wars have been started over less. It's much too complicated for us to meddle in.

"Lana. Come on," Finnian continues. "She can't mess with you like that! If you're not going to stand up for yourself, then let me stand up for you! I'll do all of it. You won't even need to know anything. Total plausible deniability."

"It's not like that." I wish so badly that I could tell Finnian about the treaty, but I know that I can't. "Jokes and pranks are one thing, but messing with my mom's happiness is another."

"Why?" he asks. "It's not like she cares about yours."

Ouch.

I stand up stiffly. All of a sudden, I don't feel like talking to Finnian. And the humming of his thoughts feels less gentle and more menacing.

"I have to go," I say.

"What?" Finnian asks as I step over the rocks and leave the cave. "What? Oh, come on, Lana!" he calls as I leave the cave. "You're overreacting!"

I am *not* overreacting. But I don't feel like talking to Finnian right now to explain just how reasonable I'm being.

All of a sudden I realize that, even though things have been kind of weird between us since I got these powers, the only person I really want to talk to is Aarav. Aarav gets how complicated things are for me and Mom. And he'd never, ever say that Mom doesn't care about me. I can't believe Finnian just said one of my worst fears out loud, casually, like it wasn't a big deal. Like it wasn't the kind of thing I don't even let myself *think*.

Is it obvious to *everyone* that Mom doesn't care about me?

Luckily, I find Aarav before I can spiral any further. He's lying under a tree in the royal fields, just looking up at the sky. But before he sees me approaching, the jumble of his thoughts resolves into words.

"I wish I could always live on land," Aarav thinks. *"I never want to go home."*

He *what*?! I stumble backward.

Aarav wants to leave home. He wants to leave *me*. Just like Mom did.

I guess everyone thinks they're better off up here on this fetid patch of dirt, far away from difficult Lana and all the problems she causes. The Lana that Aarav doesn't like very much. Lana, the *liability*.

That's it. I can't stay up here for another minute. I know Dad told me to stay on land, but I'm done following orders. If I just show up at home, it's not like he'll send me away again.

I head back to the beach, kicking off my shoes and tearing at my stupid dress as I go.

Finally, I hit the dock. I run as fast as I can, close my eyes, and leap off the edge, diving into the ocean.

CHAPTER TWENTY-ONE

As the outskirts of Clarion come into view, it's immediately obvious that something is wrong. This is not the city I left behind. The walls of the guard tower at the border are slanted, as though it could cave in at any minute. The road into the heart of Clarion is strewn with rubble. And once I make it back to my city, my *home*, I'm horrified to discover that I hardly recognize it. Now that I can actually *see* the destruction caused by the earthquake, it is so much worse than I thought.

Living in a palace is sort of a complicated thing. It's my home, yes, the only home I've known, but it's also the symbol of my country, a country I love so much. And as I swim up to the palace, I cover my mouth in horror. It may still be standing, but it's damaged in ways I hadn't prepared for. One whole section of the east wing has collapsed. The foundation at the front looks tilted, like maybe it, too, might fall at any minute. Huge chunks of the walls are missing or cracked, probably taken out by falling debris. But people are still passing through the gates, so the palace must be somewhat stable. I see a steady stream of merpeople swimming in, courtiers and politicians going about their daily business, while construction workers work to assess the damage.

I'd sort of thought people might be surprised to see me, but everyone is way too busy trying to clean up and rebuild to notice a princess who's not supposed to be here. I swim through the palace to the throne room—the floor, which once featured a map of the seven seas, is badly cracked, like the spiderwebs I've seen on land—and through the door that leads to the council room. Facing a disaster of this magnitude, Dad will probably be in here, consulting with his closest advisers.

As I suspected, he's in here—but not with his council. Instead, I recognize the wiry, wizened form of Prime Minister Telluch of the Deepest Depths. Before they see me, I get a good look at their faces, and both Dad and the Prime Minister seem deeply concerned. Now I sort of wish my mind-reading powers worked under the water the way they work on land. But here, they're back to normal, and I can only hear what Dad and Prime Minster Telluch *want* me to hear. Which, right now, is a big fat nothing.

"Lana." Dad's noticed me hovering in the doorway, and he does *not* look happy to see me. But he's not angry, either. He's exhausted. Not to mention distracted, in a way that I've never seen him before, which is so much worse.

"Your Royal Highness." Prime Minister Telluch dips his head, and I nod back. *"I thought you were visiting your mother on land?"*

"So did I." Oof, Dad's tone does *not* make me feel good about the conversation we're about to have.

"Telluch, can you give us a minute?"

"Of course, Carrack," the Prime Minister wheezes. *"Family first, of course, of course."* He starts to swim out of the room, then pauses on the threshold. *"Send word when you've considered what I've told you? The evidence . . . well, it speaks for itself."*

And with that, he leaves the room.

"Why is Prime Minister Telluch here?" I ask, bewildered. *"And what evidence was he talking about?"*

"Lana, you cannot be here right now," Dad says sternly.

"I couldn't be on land anymore, either, Dad! It was awful." I pause. How could I possibly sum it all up in a way he'd understand? *"Why can't I come home?"*

"It's unsafe."

"But there are people swimming around everywhere! Going about their daily lives! It's safe enough for our citizens, but not for me, just because I'm a princess?" I cross my arms. *"That's really unfair."*

"It's safer for them than it is for you right now."

"That makes no sense. An earthquake doesn't pick whom to crush based on which person has a tiara and which one doesn't. I'm not in any more danger than anyone else."

"You might be . . . if the earthquake wasn't just an earthquake." Dad sinks into the chair behind his desk. *"Prime Minster Telluch is claiming that Queen Fetulah orchestrated the earthquake."*

"Queen Fetulah of the Warm Seas? Finnian's mom?" This makes no sense. *"How is that even possible?"*

"There are a number of ways. Even I don't know exactly what resources the sorcerers and armorers of the Warm Seas have at their disposal. Telluch wants to commission a search party to look

for a weapon that could have caused such an unexpected seismic shift, but Fetulah is insulted by the accusation and refuses to grant him access to the Warm Seas."

"*Okay...*" I'm not super familiar with the mechanics of tectonic movement, but I guess that makes sense. "*But* why *would she do that?*"

"*He believes it was an act of war.*"

"*War?!*" I gasp. I knew there had been tension under the seas in other kingdoms outside of Clarion, specifically between the Deepest Depths and the Warm Seas. Before Queen Fetulah showed up for the summer, Dad had been traveling a lot, trying to keep the peace. And he's spent the last couple months in endless meetings. But I had no idea things were that bad. There hasn't been a war under the sea in my lifetime. I thought war was something from long ago, like krakens or sea dragons.

"*Telluch has been busy trying to prove Fetulah started the earthquake, and he arrived here a couple days ago to try to get me to side with the Deepest Depths. In case a war does break out, he wants the might of Clarion on his side. He's had a team of surveyors working around the clock to trace the origins of the earthquake, following the fault lines and cataloging the damage.*" There's a map open on Dad's desk. I don't totally understand what I'm looking at—just a series of lines tracing over the kingdoms I know well. Dad taps right at the heart of the capital of the Warm Seas. "*The evidence is fairly convincing that the earthquake originated here.*"

"*Queen Fetulah wouldn't do that.*"

"I don't think so, either, Lana." Dad shakes his head. *"But I can't say that for sure. It's possible the earthquake originated in the Warm Seas due entirely to natural causes. But it's also possible that the causes weren't natural,"* he adds darkly. *"And that's why you have to leave. I don't know whom to trust, and I'm worried you're at risk."*

"Me? But why—"

"In wartime, everyone is at risk. Especially the Crown Princess of the most powerful nation in the seven seas. Unfortunately, who you are makes you a target." Dad pulls me into a hug. *"I need you to be safe, Lana."*

"I don't want to go back." Wrapped up in Dad's arms, I feel a lot younger than fourteen. I miss the days when everything wasn't so complicated.

"You must. It's the only way I can keep you safe."

I sigh. Nobody wants me on land, and now I can't even stay in the one place I thought I could *always* come home to. I know Dad's intentions are different from Mom's, but right now, it feels like they *both* see me as a liability.

All I want to do is help, but no one wants me to.

Still, I'm not going to fight Dad on going back, even if I want to. If Clarion really has to prepare for war, the last thing I should be is a distraction. As badly as I wish I could stay here, I can't jeopardize Clarion's future. *I* am Clarion's future—its future queen—and part of keeping Clarion safe means keeping myself safe, too.

"Mom's getting married," I blurt out.

Dad's eyebrows raise just a hair. *"Hyacinth finally got the treaty ratified? Good for her. I wasn't sure she could get it done. But if anyone could, it's your mother."*

"You knew?" My jaw drops open. *"Technically, the treaty's not finalized yet, but that's not the point right now. You knew Mom was getting married the whole time?"*

"Of course. It's why she wanted you to come to the Royal Festival this year after all. She wanted you to be there."

"And, you're, um . . . okay with it?" Asking Dad about his *feelings* is a whole boatload of awkward, but I do want to make sure he's okay.

"Of course, Lana." Dad looks almost confused that I'd ask. *"Your mother and I weren't right for each other. She is a remarkable woman, and I still care for her, but that doesn't mean we should be together. Hyacinth deserves to be with someone who makes her happy,"* he says, his gaze serious as his eyes meet mine. *"Do you think this King of Fremont is that someone?"*

I think about it. I think about King Petyr's silly song. Mom reaching for his hand for comfort. The way they're almost always thinking the same thing at the same time.

"Yeah," I say, surprised to find the corners of my mouth turning upward. *"Actually, I do."*

"Good." Dad smiles. *"I'm glad to hear it."*

Wow. If *Dad* can be happy for them, then maybe I need to start looking for the positive in all of this.

I haven't found it yet. But I know I won't find it in Clarion.

Time to head back to the surface.

CHAPTER TWENTY-TWO

Miraculously, my dress is still on the dock where I left it—torn a little bit from where I struggled to get it off, but still in one piece. It's easy enough for me to operate the tanks below the docks by myself, but I had no plan B for emerging on land only to find there was no clothing in sight. I pull on my dress, shivering slightly and wishing I had a towel. If the night watchman thinks it's weird that I'm strolling into the palace all alone and soaking wet, he doesn't say so. I slink up the stairs, dry off, and collapse into my bed, grateful for some time alone with my thoughts.

The next morning, I wake up to a castle that's been transformed. The railings on the stairs into the Grand Hall are covered with white roses. Banners of white and silver silk hang from the ceilings and drape across the walls. I descend the stairs slowly, watching people scurry to and fro holding even more roses. Everyone's thinking so many things at once that I can't make sense of any of it.

Huh. That's weird. I can still hear their thoughts, even though

I went back to the sea. I'd wondered if it would take another ten days for my powers to reset. Does this mean I just have these powers forever now—I'll hear what everyone's thinking *every time* I come on land? Is the same thing true for other merpeople who have come up here? I hate not knowing what's going on inside my own brain! We have *got* to get the Royal Scholars collecting some more research on this topic. But right now, I need to know what everyone's thinking about.

"What's happening? Why is everyone rushing around?" I stop a woman who's carrying an enormous bouquet in a huge silver vase.

"Princess Hyacinth is getting married tomorrow!" she says joyfully. "We've so much to do to be ready in time!"

"Tomorrow?" I repeat, stunned. "The wedding is on? What about the treaty?"

"The other kingdoms came to an agreement this morning. The Peace and Friendship Treaty has been ratified."

Great. So I definitely I missed out on the one truly interesting piece of diplomacy that happened at the Royal Festival, bringing my ambassadorial accomplishments up to a big fat zero. And now Mom's getting married. For real.

Dad was happy for her. So I should be, too.

It's just a little harder than I thought it would be.

Well, looks like it's all wedding bells and friendship treaties on land. Now to deal with the oceans. I'm not looking forward to it, but I know I need to talk to Finnian. Even though we didn't exactly part on the best terms, I still have to let him know what's going on. He doesn't seem to have *any* idea how bad things are, and if *my* mom was being accused of being some kind of war criminal and my country was potentially on the brink of war with the Deepest Depths, I'd want to know. When Finnian left home, he thought his mom was busy with disaster relief, not preparing for battle.

If the Deepest Depths and the Warm Seas do go to war... Clarion would almost definitely get involved, too. What if Dad sided with Prime Minister Telluch *against* Queen Fetulah? What would it mean for me and Finnian to be on opposite sides of a war?

I don't even want to think about it. It seems impossible that our friendship could survive a war. My loyalty is *always* to Clarion. But the thought of losing Finnian curdles my stomach. The earthquake *has* to have been a natural disaster, nothing more. It just has to.

Finnian proves surprisingly hard to track down. I eat three waffles with maple syrup while waiting for him in the breakfast room, but he never shows. I go back upstairs after breakfast, but he's not in his room, either. And then I realize I have absolutely no idea where to look for him. What does he like to do up here, anyway? I check the Natatorium, and the garden shed, and the stables, and the cave—pretty much everywhere I've ever been with Finnian—and he's nowhere to be found. Honestly, given his propensity for escape routes, there's a good chance he's not even on the castle grounds anymore.

This is majorly weird. It's not like Finnian to disappear. Maybe he's mad at me because of our fight in the cave? But he's much more likely to cause a giant scene if he's upset about something.

My stomach twists. What if he isn't upset about anything? Maybe his disappearance has something to do with the Deepest Depths. No, that's an absurd thought. A nation of merpeople couldn't have kidnapped a prince on land.

...Right?

Part of me wonders if I should sound an alarm, but I don't want to start a panic—or possibly a war—by accusing the Deepest Depths of kidnapping with no proof. I'm sure Finnian will turn up. And just to make sure he does, I'll camp out in his room. He has to go to sleep eventually, right?

Luckily, the door's unlocked. I push it open, looking for signs that Finnian was there recently. The bed is tidily made, but that's not necessarily proof that Finnian hasn't slept in it. There's no evidence that he packed, although there's not much you can take with you if you're heading back to the sea. After a quick, guilty snoop around, I haven't found any clues as to where Finnian might be, or whether or not he went there by choice.

I guess I'll wait, then. On Finnian's bedside table, there's a small stack of books with pirate ships on the cover—left by Grandpa in all the guest bedrooms, no doubt. I grab the top one and settle into a plush reading chair by the window. There's even a cozy blanket! I pull it down around my legs, snuggling in. Comfy. So comfy I can almost forget about that whole missing-best-friend-and-threat-of-war thing.

"I can't believe I caused the earthquake." It's Finnian's voice, without a doubt. I stir awake, blinking groggily. What time is it? It's now pitch-black—I must have fallen asleep while reading this not-so-thrilling pirate adventure.

Wait a minute. Did I just hear that *Finnian* caused the earthquake?! How could he—*why* would he— My stomach flips like it's been caught in a riptide. Maybe I heard him wrong. Maybe I'm still dreaming. *"It was only supposed to cause a little rumble,"* Finnian says.

A *rumble.* I'm definitely awake, and Finnian is definitely talking about the earthquake.

How is this possible?!

"You did what?!"

Finnian screams. A light flickers on, illuminating his form in the doorway.

"Lana?" he asks incredulously. "What are you doing here?"

I stand up, the blanket sliding to the floor. I look around, but there's no one else there. Just Finnian.

"Who were you talking to?" I demand. "Where are they?"

"There's no one here, Lana," Finnian says. "It's just me."

"No, it's not. I heard you talking." Wait a minute—what am I thinking? It doesn't matter who Finnian was or wasn't talking to. Finnian *caused* the earthquake. I can't believe it. "I heard you, Finnian. Talking about starting the earthquake."

"I didn't—I...I..." And then his face crumples. "I didn't mean to, okay? Well, I *did* mean to cause the earthquake, but it wasn't supposed to do this much damage!"

"How do you even cause an earthquake?!"

"I found something in the armory in Clarion that would cause instability—"

"Like a bomb?!" I interject.

"No, not like a bomb! It was a tool used to help soldiers dig trenches back during Mer War I. It was just supposed to cause a little tiny baby bit of instability. I hid it in my trunk and took it back home with me."

"You *stole* it?" I interrupt.

"Borrowed it!" he squawks. "I was gonna give it back eventually. I swear. I wasn't even really sure I was going to use it. I just took it with me in case I needed it—and it turned out I did. So I found a fault map in the library and tossed it into a fault line that led right into the heart of Clarion." Prime Minister Telluch was right—the earthquake *did* originate in the Warm Seas. "But I underestimated the strength of the device, and it did way more damage than I thought it would."

Finnian looks miserable. If I wasn't so furious that he hurt Clarion, I could almost feel bad for him.

"Why would do you this?" I whisper.

"Because I didn't want to move to Clarion, and I *definitely* didn't want to go to school there, okay?"

"You didn't want to go to school with me?" He didn't say that specifically, but that's what I hear. I can't believe this. I was so excited to spend more time with him, and Finnian literally destroyed a city to get away from me. "Doesn't our friendship matter to you? At all?"

"Yes, Lana, of course it does!" Finnian says, exasperated. "But that doesn't mean I want to move to Clarion! I love the Warm Seas. That's my *home*. I don't care if every prince of the Warm Seas has gone to Clarion Academy since the beginning of time. That doesn't mean *I* should have to go. So I thought, if I set off the device, maybe it would cave in a roof so that school would be postponed a couple of weeks while it was being fixed, and maybe by then I would have been able to convince Mom not to send me away...."

I can't stop staring at him. How could Finnian do this?

"It wasn't supposed to be this bad, Lana. And no one was ever supposed to know."

"Then why were you just monologuing about it in the middle of your room?!"

"I wasn't. I mean, I wasn't talking about it. I was *thinking* about it. It's all I ever think about."

"That doesn't make any sense. I can't hear your thoughts."

"Yes, you can. You always could." Finnian hangs his head. He looks ashamed in a way I've never seen before. "I mean, I assume you could. I've been purposefully shutting you out, focusing my brain on humming random tunes whenever you're around so you wouldn't know what I was thinking. You just heard these thoughts because I didn't know you were here."

"So you lied to me. And not just about your thoughts. But about something so much worse."

I have to tell everyone it's not what they think—they have to call the war off!

Finnian's eyes widen with shock. He takes a couple steps back, reeling, like I just punched him.

"What?" An uncomfortable sensation crawls up my spine. Why is Finnian looking at me like that?

"I have to tell everyone," he thinks.

My mouth is hanging wide open, but no sound is coming out.

"What's going on?" We're communicating just like we would at home, reading each other's thoughts, but I've never felt further from the Finnian and Lana that we used to be. *"You can read my mind?"*

"It's day ten." His mouth is compressed into a grim line. *"I can hear* everything." I completely forgot there was a possibility that Finnian would develop powers. *"You can't tell anyone what I've done. Seriously, Lana. I'm begging you."* He drops to his knees. *"I didn't mean for it to destroy the whole school! Or anything else in Clarion. I swear."*

"I won't tell them it was you!" I promise, although I'm not sure yet exactly how I'll keep Finnian out of it. *"I'll just tell Dad it was an accident. I won't say your name at all."*

"You can't say anything, *Lana."* Finnian grabs my wrists and holds on too tight, like a barnacle stuck to the side of the dock. *"No matter what you say, they'll find out it was me. Why would they just believe that you know what happened, but ask no follow-up questions? That doesn't make any sense!"*

"I have to say something! Do you know what's going on at home, Finnian? Prime Minster Telluch thinks your mom orchestrated the earthquake as an act of war against the Deepest Depths."

"War?" Finnian's hands drop to his side, suddenly limp. *"That's not possible. Mom didn't say anything about* war. *She said they were just doing disaster relief! Poseidon help me."* Finnian balls up his fists and presses them against his eyes, almost collapsing in on himself. His thoughts are a maelstrom of terror and guilt, and I know mine aren't much clearer. "You can't tell your dad, Lana," he says aloud, his eyes wild, and he almost doesn't look like Finnian anymore. "You can't tell anyone. They'll put me in jail, or maybe force me to give up my title, or even exile me, maybe! I don't know what they'll do!"

"I have to," I say firmly. I feel sick at the thought of an exiled Finnian, but I don't see any other choice. "Otherwise, it would be a betrayal of my kingdom."

"If you do tell, it'll be a betrayal of our friendship. What about that?"

"I'm sorry, Finnian," I whisper, trying my best to be stronger than the current and steady as the tide. "This is bigger than you and me."

"What if you telling your dad *causes* a war? If your plan fails, and they trace the explosion back to me..." He trails off, his eyebrows raised meaningfully. "Technically, the earthquake *was* caused by a weapon detonated by a member of the Royal Family of the Warm Seas. Prime Minister Telluch was absolutely right. You're handing him justification for an invasion."

I hadn't even considered that possibility.

"Dad won't let that happen." I know he wouldn't. I'll tell Dad the truth—most of the truth—and then he'll fix everything. He has to. "He'll explain to everybody that it was an accident. And you'll be safe, Finnian. Because I won't tell him it was you. I promise."

"Don't make promises you can't keep, Lana."

189

Finnian sets his jaw, something in his face hardening. I swear his eyes look colder; he almost has the beady, too-focused gaze of a shark. Nothing of his usual mischief and laughter shines back at me. I shrink away from him, almost frightened by the sudden change.

"If you tell, I'll ruin Hyacinth and Petyr's wedding tomorrow and then show them the plans I made. I've been busy working on them all day. They're pretty elaborate. Masterful, even. And I'll say they were all *your* plans."

I stare at Finnian, shocked. I can't believe he would say that. I can't believe he would *do* that. But the look in his eyes tells me that he is deadly serious.

"My mom will never believe it."

"Wouldn't she?" Finnian laughs darkly. "Want to wait and find out?"

Would Mom believe Finnian over me? Would she really think I'd ruin her wedding? I know that my track record hasn't been great this year thanks to the Pirate Polo Match, but this is her *wedding*.

She can't think that little of me. She can't.

Or maybe she can. I am a *liability* after all.

I run from the room, away from this desperate stranger who looks like Finnian but acts nothing like the friend I thought I knew. I have to get to Mom. I have to tell her what Finnian is planning, have to make sure that she'll believe me and not him.

And then I have to figure out how to stop this war without getting my best friend exiled.

. . . If Finnian even *is* my best friend anymore?

For the first time in my life, I don't know what to do or who to trust. I've always been so confident in my decisions, so sure I'm doing the right thing. And yet, in this moment, I have no idea. And if you'd asked me a week ago if I trusted Finnian, my answer would have been *of course*, but now? I'm beyond confused. All I *do* know is that I need to get to Mom. I grit my teeth as I sprint away from the guest suites and all the way to Mom's room. I pause to catch my breath before knocking on Mom's door, and once again, I overhear something I wish I hadn't.

"I can't believe how much Lana hates me," Mom thinks.

Mom thinks I hate her?! I don't *hate* her. Our relationship is complicated, yes, but hate? Never. Yes, I may have said that when I was angry, but I didn't mean it. Not really. My stomach sinks. She probably *would* believe Finnian, if he told her I was planning to ruin her wedding. I mean, why wouldn't she? I've given her no reason not to expect I would do something awful like messing up her big day.

The door swings open.

"Lana?" Mom asks. She's already in her pajamas, a long blue floral dressing gown belted around her waist. "I was just coming to find you. How did you know? Did you, er, hear it?" she asks nervously.

"Nope!" I say quickly. Probably too quickly.

I can't get the words out. My mouth opens and closes a few times, but nothing comes out. The fear that she won't believe me is smothering me. "It's fine. Everything's fine. Just happened to be walking by. On a stroll. Gotta use these feet while I've got 'em."

"Oh, Lana. Clearly, everything is not fine. Do you want to talk about it?" Mom smiles sadly, shaking her head. Then I hear her think, *"She's too much like me."*

"What?!" I exclaim. *"I'm* too much like you?! I'm nothing like you!"

"We're more alike than you know," Mom says. She places a hand on the side of my face, cupping my cheek. I look up at her with surprise. "We're both headstrong, we refuse to compromise once we've made a decision, and we hate asking for help. We think we need to do everything on our own. But we don't."

When she puts it like that . . .

"It's okay to let people in, Lana. You don't have to be strong all the time. I'm trying to learn that, too." She takes her hand off my cheek, but I swear I can still feel the warmth of it. "I know I haven't always been there for you in the way you've needed me, but if there's something bothering you, you can tell me. Always."

"I . . ." I scuff my shoe along the carpet, looking down, unable to meet Mom's gaze. "I know."

I say that I know, but I don't tell her.

I can't.

CHAPTER TWENTY-THREE

"**D**ear Dad," I write, "An anonymous merpersonage has accidentally..."

Nope. Way too many follow-up questions there. I crumple up the parchment. Goodbye, draft forty-eight.

"Dear Dad," I write. "Queen Fetulah had nothing to do with..."

Feels wrong. I crumple it. Draft forty-nine.

"Dear Dad," I write. "Tell Prime Minster Telluch to stand down. There was no act of war. It was..."

I crumple draft fifty, too, and bang my head on the desk. Why is this so hard to write? Dad needs to know what happened so I can stop this war. I've been trying to write this letter all night, and I still can't get it quite right. I probably should have immediately run down to the docks to blow the summoning conch to talk to Dad, but I thought if I took the time to sit down and write things out, I could find a way to make sure Finnian wouldn't get exiled or whatever. He may have done something awful, but he's still my friend, and there's part of me that wants to protect him. I know I need to get this letter out as soon as possible, given that I have no idea how fast things are deteriorating at home, but it's so much harder than I anticipated.

Maybe it's so hard to focus because Mom is getting married today. I'm still not even sure how I feel, other than confused. I know Dad is right, and she should be with someone who makes her happy, but it still feels like this wedding is the end of something I wasn't totally ready to say goodbye to.

Think, Lana, I exhort myself. I get up from the desk and walk around. Sadly, it doesn't bring me any clarity. I rest my head against the door to my room, but the change of position isn't helping. I wish I could go for a swim right now. At home, a good long swim always clears my head. Things always make sense when there's nothing but endless blue ocean in front of me.

"I know I've had a long, storied career of pranking, but this time, I think I've outdone even myself." That's Finnian's voice. I'm sure of it. He must be walking down the hallway. *"This is a wedding people will be talking about for ages."*

What?! Finnian's already on his way to stop the wedding? I'm out of time!

"Finnian!" I dash into the hallway, calling his name. He's almost gone, disappearing down the hall. I'm about to run after him when two women, dressed in enormous ball gowns, start staring at me while they make their way down the halls, unable to hide their laughter.

"These merpeople are so strange," one of them thinks.

"It's so cute when merpeople try to understand clothes," the other one thinks.

I look down. Well, carp. I forgot that I was still in my pajamas, complete with fuzzy narwhal slippers.

"I know I'm wearing pajamas!" I shout at the laughing courtiers. "I just didn't get dressed yet, okay?"

"Unstable," one of the women thinks. *"Those merpeople are all unstable."*

"WE ARE A VERY STABLE PEOPLE WITH MORE CLASS IN ONE FIN THAN YOU LAND-LIVERS HAVE IN YOUR WHOLE BODIES!"

They're practically racing down the hall now, far enough away that I can't hear their thoughts anymore, which is probably for the best. Argh! Forget them. I have to stop Finnian so I can save the wedding that part of me still wishes wasn't happening!

The irony of this is not lost on me.

I run back into my room and grab the ball gown covered in sparkling silver flowers that the Royal Wardrobe sent over early this morning. I shuck off my pj's, pull on the gown, and dash out of my room, dodging courtiers in their finest as they stream toward the chapel.

If I'm remembering correctly from what I overheard the servants thinking about yesterday, there's a pre-wedding gathering in the courtyard, the ceremony is in the chapel, and the reception will be in the ballroom. But Finnian could be anywhere, depending on what he has planned. How can I possibly find him in time?! For lack of a better idea, I start heading to the courtyard and try my best to sort through the voices in my head, hoping I somehow pass close enough to wherever Finnian is to hear him again.

I don't hear Finnian's thoughts. But I *do* hear Aarav's name.

I look around me, trying to figure out where it's coming from. Who do I see? Visiting royalty. Dignitaries. Courtiers. And there, in a corner of the Grand Hall, there's Lady Daffodil, Lady Carnation, the Crown Prince of Caversham, and some of the other kids who were bullying Aarav back at the picnic.

They're laughing and jostling each other as they make their way to the wall of glass doors that leads out to the courtyard, and I don't like it. My instincts are telling me that something's up. Anything the Crown Prince could think about Aarav that would put a smile on his face cannot be good.

"Hey!" Their laughter quiets down as I charge toward them. There are so many people it's hard to hear what any one person is thinking. The cacophony is pounding in my head, so loud that I can barely hear *myself* think. "What's going on?"

"Nothing." The Crown Prince can barely keep a straight face as he answers me. But a glance at Lady Daffodil by his side tells me she looks guilty.

I look hard at Lady Daffodil, trying to isolate her thoughts from amid the noise, hoping she'll give me some kind of clue. *"Nothing's going on,"* she thinks, almost like she wishes it was true. *"Nothing, nothing, nothing. Absolutely nothing."*

No help. I turn to look at Lady Carnation.

"Every wedding has cake," she thinks. *"But what kind of cake? Vanilla? Chocolate? Royal Red Velvet?"*

Even less help.

"Nothing's going on," Lady Daffodil thinks again, but this time her thoughts almost sound sarcastic, like she's laughing inside her head. But not a fun laugh. Like the kind of awkward laugh that escapes at the worst possible moment, like when you're scared and a giggle tumbles out of you despite yourself. *"If Lana figures out where Aarav is,"* she thinks, *"we are in so much trouble."*

A chill courses through my body. I look down at my hands—they're shaking. Poseidon help me. What have they done with Aarav?

"Where is my brother?" I demand. Lady Daffodil's eyes dart back and forth, scared. The Crown Prince of Caversham, that miserable cretin, has the audacity to *smirk* at me. "Hey! I said, *where is my brother*?!"

Now that I'm shouting, everyone in this little clique starts thinking at once. I clap my hands over my ears, trying to make sense of what I'm hearing, but I can't.

"Tell me!" I grab on to the lapels of the Crown Prince's fancy golden jacket and shake him as hard as I can, trying to get him to say—or think—something. Anything. "Tell me! Tell me!"

"Get off!" He shoves me roughly and I stumble back a few paces, but I won't be deterred.

"What did you do to my brother?" I'm fierce as a tiger shark; it'll take more than a shove to get rid of me. I'm pulling on his jacket again, shaking him, but the buzz of thoughts is just getting louder and louder. It feels like my head is going to explode, but I have to push through to get to Aarav. "Tell me *now*. Where is my brother? What did you do to him?! What did you do?!"

"Stop that!"

Someone much bigger and stronger is pulling me off the Crown Prince. I twist around and see that it's one of the Royal Guards.

"Apologies, Your Royal Highness." He bows quickly once he sees that it's me. "Are you all right?" He eyes the Crown Prince suspiciously.

"Is *she* all right? This miserable hellion attacked me!"

"I need to see my mom," I tell the guard, ignoring the Crown Prince. "Like, as quickly as possible."

"Of course, Your Royal Highness."

"And you're coming with me." I grab on to Daffodil's arm, the yellow silk of her sleeves slippery under my fingers.

"What? Me? Why?" Daffodil's eyes widen in confusion. *"I'm in trouble,"* she thinks. *"Oh, I am in so much trouble."*

She wants me to stop thinking she's a loser? Then it's time for her to stop being one.

The crowds part easily as the guard escorts me through them, and in no time at all, we're outside a small room tucked away from the entrance to the courtyard.

"She's in there?" I ask. The guard nods, then leaves once I thank him.

But before we speak to my mom, I'm talking to Daffodil. Alone.

She looks down nervously, fiddling with her skirts. Her thoughts are so riotous I can't even distinguish one from another, but I know I can get through to her. Daffodil may act like a jerk and a bully, but I've heard her thoughts. There's part of her that wants to impress me for whatever reason. And if I can connect with that part of her, and use it to convince her to help me find Aarav, then that's all that matters.

"You're better than this, Daffodil," I say quietly. "I know you are. You're better than them. And I need you to help me." Slowly, she raises her eyes to meet mine. "Where's Aarav? Please," I beg. "I need to find him."

"It wasn't a big deal," she blurts out. "I promise. It was just supposed to be funny. I didn't think he'd be so scared...."

Scared?! What did they do to him?!

"Please, Daffodil." I'm speaking as calmly as I can, controlling my temper, just trying to get her to talk to me. "Help me find him."

"He's . . . He's over by the ocean. On the cliff, above the caves beside the beach, where the coastline gets rocky."

"Okay." I relax a tiny bit. "That doesn't sound so bad,"

"He's dangling off the cliff from a crane," Daffodil blurts out, like she's pulling out a sea urchin spine as quickly as possible to try to lessen the pain. "Hubert—the Crown Prince of Caversham—saw that they'd left out the crane from when they assembled the wedding tent, so we rolled it over to the cliffs—it was actually a lot easier to move than I thought it would be—and then Aarav—"

"I don't care how you did it!" I interrupt. This is so much

worse than I ever could have guessed. "We need to get him! Now!"

"I'm sorry," Daffodil whispers. "I didn't—"

"Mom!" I bang on the door, shouting. "Mom! Mom!"

"Lana?" Mom whips the door open. She's dressed in the most beautiful gown I've ever seen. It's made of pure white silk with long sleeves and a flowing skirt, and embroidered all over with hyacinth flowers in silver thread. There's a tiara nestled in her hair, studded with pearls and diamonds, and a lace veil cascading down her back. She looks like a princess from the fairy-tale books Grandma used to read to me when I was little. When she sees me, her face instantly becomes concerned. "What's wrong?"

"Aarav's in trouble," I tell her. "Some of those human kids have him dangling from a crane over the ocean."

"A crane?" she repeats with disbelief. "How did they— It doesn't matter." She extends her hand and I take it, even though I can't remember the last time I held her hand. "We need to get Aarav. Now."

"But what about King Petyr? The wedding?" I ask.

"The wedding will have to wait," she says fiercely. "We'll postpone it, find another day. Petyr will understand. You kids come first. Always."

Wow. Mom would really call off the wedding? I can't believe she would just do that, without a second thought.

"Guards!" Mom calls. The hallway is empty. I didn't even notice her leaving, but Daffodil must have slipped away. I'm a little disappointed—I'd hoped she might come with us to help—but at least she told me where Aarav is. That's the most important thing. And within moments of Mom's call, we're surrounded by guards. "Prince Aarav is in trouble. We need to get to the cliffs immediately."

"Muffin? Is that you?" King Petyr's voice floats from behind a nearby door. "Is everything all right?"

"Aarav's in trouble," Mom answers. "But we'll—"

"Aarav's in trouble?" King Petyr bursts through the door. "How can I help?"

"Petyr!" Mom gasps. "It's bad luck for you to see me in my dress!"

"No superstition is going to keep me from helping you rescue Aarav," Petyr scoffs. "Now, what kind of trouble are we talking?" he asks. "I'm-stuck-in-a-tree trouble, or I've-been-kidnapped-by-a-rogue-nation trouble?"

"Something in between," I answer. "Let's go!"

Mom looks like a warrior queen. She charges into the court-yard at the head of a veritable army of guards, King Petyr and me following in their wake. All the guests are standing around, sipping on champagne and nibbling hors d'oeuvres while a string quartet plays, but once everyone catches sight of Mom, the string quartet screeches to a stop and silence descends upon the party. Except, inside my head, it's louder than ever, the roar of everyone's curious thoughts almost deafening.

"The wedding is off!" King Petyr calls. "I mean, just temporarily postponed!" he shouts again, into the uproar. "We're still getting married! The treaty is on! It's just not happening today! Please help yourselves to some cake!"

From the sound of all the thoughts that follow us, I can tell no one thought that was the most reassuring speech in the history of politics, but we've got bigger problems than a postponed wedding.

We run to the cliffs as quickly as we can, flanked by the Royal Guards. These land-livers will never understand how deeply rooted the fear of heights is for all merfolk. Or if they *did* understand, then this was an act so unconscionably cruel that I *hope* Grandpa throws them all in the dungeon—including Daffodil.

As we head toward the coast, I see a wooden crane sticking out over the ocean, and dangling from its hook is *my little brother*. It looks like the rope is hooked into his pants somehow. Will his pants hold until we get there?! Obviously, Aarav is a very strong swimmer—and as soon as he hit the water, he'd have a tail again—but I can't imagine how terrified he'd be if the rope snapped and he plummeted down, down, down.

I can't imagine how terrified he must be right now.

Once we make it to the base of the crane, the Royal Guards take over. They swing the jib of the crane back around, and one of them climbs up, removes the hook from the belt loops on Aarav's pants, and carries him to safety, setting him gently down on the ground.

Aarav is so scared I can't hear words in any of his thoughts, just panicked noise.

Mom is by his side faster than seems humanly possible,

wrapping him up in a huge hug. I run to join them, curling myself around Aarav's back, so we make a little hugging family circle.

"It's okay, Aarav," Mom croons, rocking him back and forth. "It's okay. You're safe now."

Suddenly, Aarav's head pops up from our huddle.

"The wedding!" he cries. "Oh, Mom, I ruined your wedding! You're in your gown, and, and—Petyr!" he exclaims, noticing King Petyr standing behind us. "You're not supposed to see her before the wedding! It's bad luck! Grandma told me that was an important land-liver wedding tradition. Oh no, I'm so sorry. I ruined everything."

"You ruined *nothing*," Mom says fiercely.

"Nothing to apologize for, kiddo," King Petyr says. "We're just glad you're okay." He holds out his hand, and then he and Aarav execute a fairly elaborate secret handshake, heavy on the dance moves. It even puts a little smile on Aarav's face, and I find that I'm grateful that King Petyr is here.

While Mom and I walk Aarav back to the palace, King Petyr goes to see if he can reassure any visiting dignitaries who haven't dispersed that everything is fine with the treaty.

It's already dark, and way too late for the wedding to start today. So instead, in no time at all, Aarav is tucked into bed in his pajamas, sipping cocoa from a mug emblazoned with the royal crest of Clarion, a plate of warm chocolate chip cookies on his nightstand. Sitting cross-legged on Aarav's covers, I reach over to help myself to a bite—because I may not have been traumatized, but even I cannot resist the allure of a warm cookie.

"I can't believe they did that to me," Aarav says, staring mournfully into his mug. I don't need to read his thoughts to tell how upset he is.

"How did they even manage it?" I ask.

"I was on my way to the wedding. I wanted to get there early, you know? Rehearse my ring-bearer walk one last time." That is so Aarav. "But on my way to the chapel, I ran into the Crown Prince of Caversham and Daffodil and that whole crowd. And they told me there was an injured seagull over on the cliffs—"

"An injured *seagull*?!"

"Yeah. With a broken wing. So I followed them over to see if we could help it. And they kept saying it was hurt, and lying in the grass by the crane. And when I bent over to look at it, they hooked the crane into my belt loop. And the next minute, I was up in the air."

"That is messed up." I shake my head. Mom reaches over to squeeze Aarav's leg, a sympathetic look on her face.

"Yeah . . . I can't believe anyone would do this. That was more than stupid kids' bullying; that was . . ." Words seem to fail him. "I didn't know people could be so cruel," he says eventually.

My first instinct is to say, "Yeah, land-livers blow bubbles, like I've been saying all along," but I bite it back. The idea of my optimistic little brother giving up on humanity as a whole is too much, even for me—and I have been on record as pretty anti-humanity for a long, long time.

"Humans can be really cruel," I say instead. "But they can

also be really wonderful. Von has been a really good friend to you. And Grandma and Grandpa are humans, and they might be even nicer than you are." He laughs at this. "And . . . And Mom and Petyr dropped everything to help you. Which makes them pretty amazing, too."

I feel a little too shy to look directly at Mom, but out of the corner of my eye, I can see her smiling at me.

"Sure, there isn't a single person who's as good as any merperson," I say jokingly, "but that's not *their* fault. . . ."

"Lana," Mom warns as Aarav laughs. "That kind of rhetoric caused a war between Clarion and the Hills that lasted for nearly a century."

War.

In my worry over Aarav, I'd forgotten all about Finnian and the earthquake and whatever's brewing under the waves between the Warm Seas and the Deepest Depths! As soon as I make sure Aarav is okay, I'm going to tell Mom what Finnian did so she can help me get a message to Dad.

And I'm going to tell her everything. If I learned anything from all my failed attempts at writing that letter, there's no way to stop this war without telling people it was Finnian's fault— even if it *was* an accident. I can't protect him any longer, and I shouldn't. He didn't mean to hurt anybody, but that doesn't change the fact that he did.

And there's Finnian's plan to stop the wedding! I still don't even know what it is! Who knows what kind of booby traps are lurking around the castle, waiting for Mom and King Petyr?

"It was so scary, Lana," Aarav whispers while Mom folds his

clothes and hangs them over the chair for the servants to take to the laundry tomorrow morning.

"I know." I put down the last couple bites of my cookie so I can grab his hand. "I can't even imagine how awful it was. But you survived. And you were so, so brave. I don't think I could have handled this nearly as well as you're coping."

"Of course you could have. You're the bravest person I know."

"I'm not so sure about that." Recently, none of my behavior has felt particularly brave.

"Do you want me to stay with you tonight?" Mom asks, coming over to smooth Aarav's covers. "I can sleep in the chair. I don't mind."

"I'm okay." Aarav puts his mug on the side table. He's blinking sleepily, his eyes closing. "I think I'm just going to fall asleep."

"If you're sure . . ."

Aarav nods, yawning. He snuggles deeper under the covers, cuddling his pillow. And he's snoring before Mom shuts the door quietly behind us.

There's nothing like pure terror to really exhaust you, I guess.

We're alone in the hallway, Mom and I, and I realize she's still in her wedding gown. I totally forgot she was supposed to get married today.

"I can't believe you ditched your wedding."

"Of course I did." Mom looks like she can't believe I'd think she *wouldn't* ditch her wedding. "You two mean more to me than anything else on the planet. There is nothing I wouldn't do for you. *Nothing*," she adds fiercely.

"Then . . . why did you leave us?" I ask in a small voice. I didn't even mean to. It just kind of slipped out.

Mom sinks to the floor, resting her back against the wall. She pats the bit of carpet next to her, and I sit down, folding my knees under the huge skirt of this ridiculous ball gown.

"I didn't leave Clarion because I wanted to leave *you*, Lana. You know how . . . You know how much you love Clarion?" I nod. "That's how I feel about the Hills. I love running the way you love swimming. I love the warmth of the sun the way you love the cool depths of the sea. And I found, after seven years in the ocean, that I missed it too much to live without it."

I consider this. I can't imagine never returning to the sea; it would be like slowly suffocating.

"That's why I see myself in you, Lana," Mom says. "In your fierce love of where you come from. And, if I'm being honest, in your headstrong nature and unwillingness to compromise, too." She smiles. Well, when she puts it like that, I *can* see the similarities between us. "And, Lana, I am so, so glad I married your father, because I have you and Aarav. The two of you are the most important things in the whole world to me."

An unexpected warmth spreads through my chest, but even with her kind words, I can't quite meet Mom's eyes.

"Then why do we only see you once a year?"

"You're right; it's not enough. I should have made more of an effort to spend time with you and Aarav after the divorce. But the two of you—you especially—seemed so much happier under the sea with your father. I didn't want to mess things up.

I was worried that if I kept popping under the sea to see you, or demanding you come up here, it would have made things even more difficult and strained."

"It might have," I answer honestly. I was really, really mad at Mom when she left. Even if she had come to visit, I probably would have refused to see her.

"But I'd like to spend more time with you going forward. If that's okay with you?" Mom asks hopefully. "And I am so, so sorry I didn't tell you about the wedding. I should have. I was so focused on keeping it a secret for the sake of the treaty. But I know that I could have trusted you, and I wish I had."

"Thank you." No matter where we go from here, it's a relief to hear that she believes in me. "And yeah, I mean yes," I say. "I'd like to spend more time with you, too."

And I'm surprised to find that I mean it.

But now I have to stop a war.

Why is it so hard to tell Mom what Finnian did?

"Hyacinth!"

King Petyr bursts into the hall, and he is covered from head to toe in swirls of colorful paint.

"Oh, Hyacinth!" Petyr is clearly distraught. "The chapel is ruined!" he cries.

"What happened?" Mom scrambles to her feet, and I jump up after her.

"Ugh. I know what," I say. Finnian happened. We're staring at the evidence of his grand prank.

Mom looks at me. I look at her. We both look at her

multicolored groom, and neither of us can help it: We immediately start giggling.

"What's so funny?" King Petyr asks, confused

"Lovebug, come here." Mom takes King Petyr's hands. I follow as she leads him gently to a full-length mirror edged in gilt a bit farther down the hall.

"Oh . . . my."

King Petyr considers himself in the mirror. He looks himself up and down and eventually . . . bursts out laughing.

His laugh is so loud and so infectious, it sets me and Mom off again. We're laughing so hard we're practically wheezing. I'm doubled over, wiping tears from my eyes, when Mom asks again, "How on earth did this *happen*?"

"Finnian made plans to spoil your wedding," I say, now feeling like things aren't quite so funny. "That's why I came to talk to you. Last night. But he was going to say it was all *my* idea, and I was worried you wouldn't believe me—"

"Of course I would have believed you," Mom says, shocked. "Lana. You have a good heart, and you are not a liar. I know you would never do something like that."

"Oh. Um. Thank you." And there's that unexpected warmth spreading through my chest again. I can't believe that Mom so easily sees the best in me, just like that. Even after I messed up so badly at the Pirate Polo Match. "But that's why I was coming to find you—to stop Finnian from ruining the wedding. But then I overheard those kids thinking about Aarav, and I totally forgot. . . ."

"Thank you, Lana." Mom squeezes my hand. "I know this wedding hasn't exactly been easy on you...." She and Petyr exchange a glance. Honestly, most of the time, it seems like *they're* the ones who can read each other's minds. "But the fact that you tried to stop Finnian and save our wedding means a lot to me."

"I want you to be happy, Mom. Really. And I can tell...I can tell that King Petyr makes you happy." The two of them are smiling so widely it almost looks painful.

Now it's time for me to do something I should have done a long time ago. "King Petyr, I'm sorry I was so awful to you at the beginning of the Royal Festival. There's no excuse for the way I acted."

"It's okay, Lana," he says. "I get how complicated this must be for you. I really do. My dad remarried when I was eleven, and I was convinced my stepmother was Wicked-with-a-capital-*W*. I kept searching her room for poison apples." He chuckles. "But once I got to know her, I was glad she was part of our family. And I hope, one day, you'll be glad that I'm part of your family, too."

King Petyr scoops me up into a huge hug, and then Mom joins in, and I find myself in the second group hug of the day.

"So how did Finnian do it?" I ask gruffly, disentangling myself. There's only so much group hug time I can take. "Did he stuff a cannon full of paint or something?"

"Less violent, more advance planning," King Petyr says. "It seems that he rigged dozens of paint-filled water sacs to explode during the ceremony. When I went to talk to the organist, I must have tripped the ropes—every single paint sac exploded on me as I made my way up the aisle."

"Your poor suit." Mom reaches out to touch his sleeve, which is now mostly purple. "The Royal Seamstresses spent ages working on it."

"The Royal Seamstresses will get over it." King Petyr waves his hand, unconcerned. "The only thing that matters is that Aarav is safe," he says. "But someone is *really* going to have to clean up the chapel before we actually get married."

Mom starts laughing again. And before I know it, I'm laughing, too, and then King Petyr joins in, his big booming laugh almost shaking the walls.

King Petyr has a *great* laugh.

I can understand why Mom would want to be with someone who laughs like that.

They look so happy, I can't believe I'm about to ruin the mood. But I know it's the right thing to do.

"Mom, I have to tell you something." I take a deep breath. "Finnian caused the earthquake that destroyed Clarion."

Mom's eyebrows shoot up to her hairline. Petyr emits a surprised little cough.

"That's not possible, Lana," Mom says. "He's a child. There's no way he could have—"

"Hyacinth." Petyr lays a calming hand on her arm. "Let's hear what Lana has to say."

"He did it, Mom. I heard him confess. But it was an accident! I mean, yes, he did intentionally cause the earthquake. But he only wanted to create a little disturbance to get school shut down so he didn't have to come to Clarion Academy. He never meant to cause this much damage. Or to hurt anybody. And he certainly didn't mean to cause a war between the Warm Seas and the Deepest Depths."

Mom's mind is whirling away, thinking of next steps. *"War,"* she thinks. *"I knew this was a possibility, but Carrack had hoped to stop things before they got to this point."*

"Have you told your father yet?" she asks eventually.

"No. I tried to...." I feel terrible I didn't do anything about this earlier, but it was so hard. Trying to protect Finnian was an impossible task. "I drafted fifty letters trying to tell him. But I just couldn't do it." Mom takes my hand in hers, and it helps. "I hate ratting out my friend, and I *know* he didn't mean for things to go this far, but what he did was dangerous. So many merpeople could have been hurt. So many merpeople still could be hurt."

"It's okay, Lana," Mom says soothingly. "You're brave for telling the truth. I'm proud of you."

Mom's words should be comforting, but coming clean isn't the relief I thought it would be. I know I did the right thing, but I can't shake this nagging unease that I'm betraying Finnian.

"We need to tell Dad, though. I know that."

"I'll write to your father immediately," Mom says decisively.

"No." I shake my head. "I'm the ambassador. It should come from me."

Mom looks surprised but nods. "Of course. I'll write to Queen Fetulah of the Warm Seas."

"And I'll get a message to Prime Minster Telluch of the Deepest Depths," Petyr offers.

"We can stop this war before it starts, Lana," Mom says.

"What about Finnian?" I'm almost afraid to ask.

"I'll have the Royal Guards find him. Then Finnian will be sent home to his mother. I'm sure Queen Fetulah will want to deal with him herself."

That's fair. But, boy, I would not want to be in Finnian's fins when he gets back to the Warm Seas.

While Mom and Petyr compose their letters, I go to do what I should have in the first place: blow the summoning conch. And after I give the advance guardsman a brief recap of what's happened, it doesn't take long for Dad himself to rise to the surface.

"Lana." Dad emerges from the waves, water streaming from his beard. "Isn't it past your bedtime?"

"Diplomacy doesn't keep regular hours, Dad."

He chuckles, then swims right up to the edge of the dock.

"What happened, Lana?" he asks gently.

I tell him everything. About Finnian stealing the device from our armory and setting off the earthquake on purpose—though definitely not intending to cause a war. Dad listens, really listens, until I'm finished.

"It doesn't feel as good as I thought it would." I take a seat, folding my legs up under the skirt of my ball gown.

"What doesn't?"

"Doing the right thing." I lean forward, resting my chin in my hands. "I know I needed to tell on Finnian. If I hadn't, the

Deepest Depths might have invaded the Warm Seas! But I hate feeling like I betrayed him."

"This is the first in a long line of difficult decisions you'll have to make when *you* become queen," Dad says. "Doing the right thing doesn't always feel good. It's rarely easy. And sometimes what the right thing *is* isn't clear. But today, you put your people first. Even when it was hard. And that's how I *know* you were meant to be the next queen of Clarion." Dad rests his arms on the ladder up to the dock. "I am so, so proud of you, Lana."

"Thanks, Dad." It *does* help, hearing Dad say that. I knew being a queen wouldn't be easy. But I understand so much better now just how hard it's going to be.

And I know I can do it.

"And Finnian will be okay," he promises. "I'm sure he won't have the most fun couple of months, but he'll be okay."

"So he won't be exiled? Or forced to renounce his title?"

"No, no, nothing like that," Dad says. "I'm sure of it." I don't know *how* he's so sure, but Dad's never lied to me before, so I know he'll make sure Finnian is safe. "Now, I have a war to stop. And you should get some sleep. Good work today, Lana." He pushes off from the dock. "I'm sure the council will be eager to hear your full report when you return to the ocean."

When I return to the ocean. That's all I've wanted to do, ever since I got here. But as I watch Dad disappear under the waves, I know there's still so much I need to accomplish on land.

First things first: I have *got* to see what Finnian did to that chapel.

CHAPTER TWENTY-FOUR

"It looks like ..." Mom says, struggling to think of an analogy. "It looks like ..."

"Like a bag of jelly beans exploded," Petyr finishes for her. When I get to the chapel, Mom and Petyr are already standing there. The normally sedate space has been transformed into a riot of color. The back pews are mostly orange and blue, the front ones are mostly yellow and red, and the altar, where Mom and Petyr would have stood, is a particularly bright blend of purple and green.

"What's a jelly bean?" I ask.

"A sugary little candy shaped like a bean," Petyr explains. "They're mostly fruit-flavored, but sometimes you get weird ones. Anyway, they come in all kinds of colors in one bag, and if they exploded, I imagine it would look—"

"Exactly like this," I finish for him. The chapel is empty, apart from the organist, who is carefully cleaning the organ with a wet rag, trying to get all the paint off. In silence, the three of us look around the ruined chapel, sticky with paint and splashed with every color of the rainbow.

"You know what I think?" Mom says. "I think the paint job is . . . rather festive."

She smiles, her eyes alight with mischief.

"Do you think . . . ?" Petyr asks.

"Even though it's so late?"

"Under the moonlight? Could be romantic."

"Will everyone have left?"

"None of the really important people."

"So should we . . . ?"

"Absolutely."

I can hear what they're thinking, but even if I couldn't, it's obvious: Paint or no paint, no matter how late it is, my mom and King Petyr are getting married tonight—right here, right now.

"Barbara!" King Petyr calls. The organist looks up, blinking through paint-spattered spectacles. "Start warming up! The wedding is back on!"

"What about Aarav?" I ask.

"Wake him up!" Mom says. "Don't worry; I promise we won't start without him."

As Mom and Petyr go to wake any royal guests who are still around, I run back upstairs to Aarav's room. There's no response when I knock, so I let myself in and gently shake Aarav's shoulder.

"What's wrong?" Aarav sits bolt upright, his hair sticking out in every direction. Right—the last time someone shook him awake in the middle of the night, Mom told him an earthquake had hit Clarion.

"Nothing's wrong!" I reassure him. "Everything's great. Don't worry. But Mom and Petyr are getting married. Like, right now. Also Finnian almost caused a war. But we stopped it. So we're all good on that front. "

"The wedding's back on!" Aarav hops out of bed like his pajamas are on fire and runs into his closet. I'm not sure if he didn't hear the part about the war, or if it's just not his priority. "I'm not ready! I can't go like this!"

"Put on anything!" I laugh. "It's all getting covered with paint anyway!"

Aarav pops a quizzical head out of the closet.

"I'll explain on the way." I wave my hands dismissively.

With impressive speed, Aarav emerges from the closet dressed in a shimmery silver suit that probably worked really nicely with Mom's original color concept. It looks like it's made out of the same material as my dress, although even from walking through the chapel, my dress now has some sticky paint splotches on it.

As we make our way through the halls of the palace, I fill Aarav in on everything that's happened while he was sleeping. By the time Aarav and I get back to the chapel, there are more royal guests than I expected to see there, and they don't seem to mind in the slightest that their fancy frocks and dazzling jackets are now covered with paint. In fact, it looks like some of the staff has set out *more* buckets, and everyone is happily painting themselves, each other, and any blank space they can find in the chapel. We even see a bunch of guys with "H+P 4EVA" painted on the back of their suit jackets.

"Lana! Aarav!" Mom is waving at us from the back of the chapel, tucked into a little alcove. We scoot over and join her.

Okay, I know, I was initially thrown off by this wedding, but I can't help it: I've gotten swept up in all the excitement.

And King Petyr is actually pretty great.

"I'm so glad the two of you are here." Mom folds us into a hug. "Today wouldn't be nearly as special without you."

I smile. Maybe this group hug thing is growing on me a little.

"Did you finish your letters?" I ask.

"Already given to the advance guardsman of Clarion. Who was able to report that, thanks to you, your father had already gotten Prime Minister Telluch to stand down. It'll take my letter a little longer to reach Queen Fetulah in the Warm Seas, but I would imagine she'll swim up to collect Finnian within a few days."

"The Deepest Depths had to stand down? Wait a minute—that thing you said about the war was real?!" Aarav asks.

"It was almost *too* real. I'll fill you in later," I promise.

"For now, let's just celebrate." Mom smiles. "However, we are going to have to do something about your clothes." She reaches a hand into the nearest bucket and splashes me with paint.

"Hey!"

I immediately retaliate; then she splatters Aarav, and within moments we're all perfectly pink, messy as can be but having the time of our lives. I can't remember the last time I had this much fun with my mom.

Suddenly, a series of chords on the organ interrupts our paint fight.

"That's Barbara!" Mom calls. "And it's our cue! Lana...a flower girl doesn't feel quite right for this wedding, but I'd love to have you involved. How do you feel about being a paint girl?"

Involved in Mom's wedding. I take a deep breath. But even with how complicated these last couple days have been, I know exactly what I want to do.

"I'd love to."

Grandly, I make my way down the aisle, flinging paint as I go. I've never been a flower girl before—I've never even been a bubble girl back home—but I have a feeling this is a lot more fun. I take my seat in an empty chair right in the front row and watch Aarav walk down the aisle with a surprisingly clean pillow holding two gold rings. When he's done, Aarav takes a seat next to me, but almost as soon as he sits, the music changes and everyone stands.

There's Mom, walking down the aisle. Her formerly immaculate dress is covered with messy, dripping paint, but she looks beautiful. She's so happy she's almost glowing. Actually, *everyone* in the church is so happy that their thoughts have formed a warm, wonderful buzz in my mind.

The ceremony is really nice. There's lots of laughter and crying, but the good kind—only happy tears for the King and new Queen of Fremont. When the minister pronounces them husband and wife and they kiss, everyone cheers so loudly it's a wonder the roof doesn't fly off. Amid all the applause, even more paint rains down from the ceiling, splashing the guests as they dance in the pews to the recessional, Mom and King Petyr twirling their way down the aisle, splattered with every color of the rainbow.

Finnian may have unintentionally started a wedding trend that'll be all the rage in the Hills for the next fifty years. I imagine any wedding without paint is going to look pretty dull now.

Aarav and I follow the flow of guests into the ballroom for the reception. Suddenly, we both realize we're starving. Luckily, waiters are circling with all kinds of tiny foods on trays. We're each about six deep-fried mac-and-cheese bites in when a woman takes the stage at the end of the ballroom, tapping a knife against a glass until she gets everyone's attention.

"And now," the woman onstage says, "put your hands together for . . . Royal Pain!"

The crowd goes *wild*. I had completely forgotten about King Petyr's band. Or, I guess, it never occurred to me that they might perform at the wedding.

"Come on!" Aarav grabs my hand and pulls me through the crowd, bobbing and weaving until we're right up by the stage.

King Petyr is in the front with his guitar, next to the lead singer. There's also a guy on drums, a woman on piano, and another woman playing the bass. They're all equally covered in paint.

"Everybody in the Hills . . . how are you feeling tonight?!" the lead singer asks. The crowd screams in response. "Can we feel the love in this ballroom?!" The crowd screams again, even louder than before. "Petyr, man," he continues, turning to King Petyr on his right, "we all love you so much. And, Hyacinth, we're so glad Petyr found you. We love you guys together. Hyacinth, welcome to the Royal Pain family."

"Thanks, man." King Petyr envelops his friend in a hug. "This next song goes out to a very special lady." He winks at the audience. "It's called 'Hyacinth.' Take it away, Duke!"

The duke on the drums raises his drumsticks above his head and shouts, "One! Two! A-one-two-three-four!"

Mom is at the front of the stage, fangirling so hard that it would be *extremely* embarrassing if it wasn't also kind of cute. And actually, it makes sense because, much to my great surprise, Royal Pain kind of . . . rocks.

"They're pretty good!" I shout to Aarav over the music, astonished.

"I know!" Aarav is jumping up and down, waving his hands in the air, doing all kinds of uncoordinated kicks. Having legs has really not improved his dancing. "Come on, Lana! Dance with me!"

And for the first time ever on land, I do.

CHAPTER TWENTY-FIVE

Apparently, Mom and Petyr were supposed to leave right away for their honeymoon on one of the islands in the Warm Seas. But the honeymoon is on pause until Finnian can be safely returned to his mother—and until Mom and Petyr are sure there's no lasting instability in the Warm Seas.

And speaking of instability in the Warm Seas, there's something I have to do. No matter how much I wish I didn't. I've put it off long enough. Even though I've never been so tired in my life—and after staying up all night dancing, I'm definitely not in the best headspace for a difficult conversation—I owe it to Finnian to at least talk to him.

I take an extra-fortifying bite of maple-syrup-drenched waffles, then think, with a pang, of Finnian bringing me waffles in my room when I felt overwhelmed. Even though he kept something huge from me, something awful, I know that he isn't a bad merperson, and the harm he caused was totally accidental. After everything we've been through together, I can't let him return to the sea without at least saying goodbye. And explaining why I had to tell on him.

Thankfully, Finnian hasn't been sent to the dungeons. I know they're a lot nicer than they used to be, thanks to the prison-reform campaign Mom led last year, but they're still, you know, dungeons. I'm glad he's just being kept in his room, but when I arrive there and see the guard stationed outside his door, I get a pit in my stomach.

"Can I see Finnian?" I ask the guard.

"Of course, Your Highness." Luckily, all the guard is thinking about is when he can have lunch. Boring, everyday thoughts have become such an unexpected relief. I never would have guessed how much I'd enjoy hearing about this rando guard's favorite kinds of sandwiches.

"Finnian, it's me," I call, knocking on the door. "Lana. Can I come in?"

"Sure." I hear the sound of something hitting the door. "If the prisoner is allowed to have visitors."

The guard steps aside to let me in. Now he's wishing he had a different detail. According to his thoughts, Finnian is usually even sassier than this.

No surprise.

Finnian is sitting on the floor, a small rubber ball in his hands. As soon as I shut the door behind me, he bounces the ball against it, catching it neatly with one hand.

"I'm surprised you came to see your friend, the war criminal." The ball bounces again, thumping against the door. *"Isn't talking to me an act of high treason for perfect Princess Lana?"*

This time, when the ball bounces back, I snatch it out of the air and catch it myself.

It's so weird hearing his thoughts again now that he's not hiding them from me with his humming. And it's even weirder knowing he can hear *all* my thoughts, too.

"*I'm sorry I got you in trouble.*" I sit down on the floor next to him. "*But I didn't have a choice. You have a good heart, Finnian, but you did something incredibly reckless. There were* bound *to be consequences. And even though you're mad at me right now, I know that deep down, you know how much your friendship means to me. There's almost nothing I wouldn't do for you.*"

Finnian snorts, thinking, "*Yeah, right.*"

I sit there for a moment, trying to keep my mind blank. It's harder than I thought it would be!

"*I would have covered for you, Lana,*" he thinks. "*That's what* your *friendship means to me. If you were the one who was in trouble, no matter what you did, I wouldn't have told anyone.*"

"*It wasn't fair of you to expect me to do that for you,*" I counter. It doesn't matter what Finnian would or wouldn't have done if our situations were reversed. He was asking the impossible. "*Not when the stakes are this high. This wasn't the bubble prank. This was a lot bigger.*"

"*I know it's big. Do you have any idea how much trouble I'm in? All because you told on me.*"

"*I didn't want to, but I had to. And it wasn't just because so much of Clarion was destroyed—I understand that was an accident—but I had to say something because if I didn't, the Deepest Depths was going to go to war with the Warm Seas. Your home, Finnian."* He seems to slump into himself. *"I know you love the Warm Seas just as much as I love Clarion."*

"The Warm Seas is a lot better than Clarion," he thinks grumpily, but I can tell he's joking. *"It's warmer, for one thing. The water's clearer. We've got more colorful plants. Better music. We actually know how to put spice on food—"*

"Exactly what I mean. You love your home." I cut him off, nicely, before he can recite the entirety of the Warm Seas' Board of Tourism official pitch. *"Which is why I know you understand why I told on you. If Prime Minister Telluch declared war, the Warm Seas could have been destroyed, way worse than Clarion."*

Right now, Finnian is thinking about a coral reef. He's picturing it so clearly, I can almost see the pink coral and the brilliantly colored fish darting through them. This must be his version of the anemone park, back home in the Warm Seas.

"And even more merpeople could have—would have—gotten hurt. Died. I couldn't let that happen, and I couldn't let you be responsible for that." I reach out and take his hand. He doesn't push me away. *"I know it feels like things are bad now. But it could have been so, so much worse. I just wanted to keep things from getting worse—for the Warm Seas, for Clarion, and for you."*

"I'm sorry, Lana." Much to my surprise, Finnian pulls me into a hug. *"I'm sorry I hurt Clarion. And I'm sorry I asked you to cover up for me. I let things get so much worse than they needed to be."*

"It's okay." I hug him back.

"I was just scared."

"I don't blame you." I hug him a bit tighter. I know it took a lot for him to admit that. *"I would have been, too."*

"I thought perfect Princess Lana was never scared." He pulls away and looks at me, grinning. *"I thought she was so brave, she ate sharks for breakfast and flossed her teeth with their bones."*

"It would be pretty hard to floss with a shark bone. Seeing as they're all cartilage."

"Spoken by someone who's regularly eating sharks." We laugh, the sound sudden in the quiet room. *"Man, this mind-reading thing is no joke."* He shakes his head. *"It's . . . weird, suddenly finding out what everyone actually thinks about you."*

"I know." Once you understand how much your actions affect everyone, it's hard to do anything carelessly.

"Sheesh, Lana!" Finnian grins. *"No need to tell me the moral of the fable. I figured it out on my own."* Oh, right. He can hear me! *"Don't worry. I'm turning over a new tide. Time for a pranking hiatus."*

"Probably a good idea."

Finnian smiles at me, but then he drops his head into his hands.

"I can't believe I have to go home and face my mom. She's going to be so mad. Everyone's going to be so mad. All of the ocean is going to hate me."

"You can face her. You can face all of them. You'll apologize, and own up to your mistakes, and work to make it right. Because you're brave, too, Finnian."

"I don't know about that, Lana. But I'm going to try to be." He sits up and looks at me, his eyes clear. *"You sure you don't want*

to come talk to my mom for me?" he thinks hopefully. And there's the spark of mischief I recognize.

I laugh and squeeze his hand. He squeezes back.

"You've got this, Finnian."

And I know he does.

CHAPTER TWENTY-SIX

The longest Royal Festival in the history of *ever* has finally come to an end, and now that Dad, Queen Fetulah, and Prime Minister Telluch are clear on the *actual* source of the earthquake, it's safe for Aarav and me to return to the ocean. But for once, I don't feel ready to go.

The two of us stand on the beach with Mom and Petyr and Grandma and Grandpa and some of the royal staff, waiting for Dad and his retinue to appear. A light breeze blows over us, the salty smell of the ocean comforting as a hug.

"Can't we just get out of here already?" Aarav asks.

Boy, I can't believe how much things have changed. Aarav and I have totally switched places.

"I need a break," he continues. "A break from these land-livers, and the hot sun, and all the smells, and ... and ..."

"And the heights?" I supply.

"Especially the heights," he agrees. "Don't get me wrong, Mom and Petyr's wedding was *awesome*. But everything else?" He shudders. "Let's just say I'm ready to go back to the depths, where things are safe. You were *so* right about everything on land, Lana."

"I wasn't right about *everything*." As much as I love when people tell me I'm right, I can't agree with all of it this time. I look to my right, where Grandma is bustling around making sure everyone has a cold glass of lemonade and Grandpa is joking with some of the Royal Guards. I look to my left, where Mom and Petyr are holding hands and smiling at each other. Mom is definitely not the cold, heartless sea monster I made her out to be. And Petyr is maybe the nicest king on land. I'm so glad he married Mom.

And, perhaps most importantly, Royal Pain *rules*.

We hear the sound of a conch shell, and everyone looks to the ocean. Following that first blast from the Royal Trumpeter, merpeople begin to emerge from the ocean. I see guards and courtiers and more musicians—and, finally, there he is.

"Dad!" Aarav shouts joyfully. After quickly hugging Grandma and Grandpa goodbye, he starts running toward the dock, eager beyond belief to change his legs for a tail. Mom, Petyr, and I follow. By the time we get to the end of the dock, Dad is there waiting, bobbing gently in the water.

I'm so happy to see him, I almost change my mind. But I know what I need to do.

"Aarav. Lana." I can tell how much Dad missed us. "It is so good to see you. I'm so happy to have you home."

"Me too!" Aarav is doing a little excited jig, bouncing up and down. "Seriously, Dad. You have no idea. *No* idea."

"Congratulations on the wedding, Hyacinth and Petyr," Dad

says. "I heard it was quite the affair to remember," he adds, eyes twinkling.

"Thanks, Carrack," Petyr says earnestly.

Looking at Petyr and Mom all snuggled up together, I realize that Dad hasn't been on a date since . . . ever. I'm sure it's hard to have much of a social life when you're a king, but if King Petyr can make it happen, I'm sure Dad can. Maybe it's about time Dad also finds a special someone who makes him happy, too.

Maybe I can help.

Come to think of it, I'm pretty sure Kishiko and Umiko's mom isn't dating that geologist anymore. . . .

"Okay, so, bye, Mom. Bye, Petyr." Aarav gives them hugs in quick succession. He's in a such a hurry to get in the water it's almost funny. "Ready, Lana? Let's shake a tail fin."

"Lana?" Dad says, confused. It's almost like he can sense my hesitation—or read my mind. "Are you ready to say your goodbyes?"

"I'm not coming." Dad's bypassed confused and gone straight into full-blown shock. "I mean, I'll come home eventually, of course, but for right now, I want to stay."

I dart a glance sideways. First, Aarav's jaw drops, but then he shoots me an encouraging smile, and thinks, *"Of* course.*"* It gives me the strength I need to explain to Dad *why* I'm staying.

I need to make sure Dad knows I'm not rejecting him, or Clarion, or the mermaid half of myself. I would *never* reject those things. They're the most important part of me. But they're not the only part of me, even though I've acted like they were for most of my life.

"I just need to learn more about my human side right now," I say. "And I want to get to know my mom and King Petyr better, too." Mom squeezes my shoulder, and I can feel how much she loves me—no mind reading required. I can, however, hear King Petyr thinking, *"Don't cry in front of Carrack. Don't cry in front of Carrack."*

What a total fluffy seal pup he is.

"And I want to get this new power of mine under control, too," I add. Spending time with Mom and Petyr is priority number one, but it would be nice to figure out a coping mechanism for being around crowds so my brain doesn't always feel like it's going to explode.

"I understand, Lana," Dad says. I can tell he's a little sad that I'm not coming back right now, but that he supports me 100 percent. And that's what really matters. "So just Aarav will come home right now."

"But I can come back to the Hills to visit more while Lana's staying here, right?" Aarav asks.

"Of course," Dad confirms.

"I may be over land . . . but I'm never over you," Aarav whispers. I really do have the best little brother in the world.

"I think we need to spend at least a month with Clarion's newest ambassador," Mom says. I look up at her, surprised. "The treaty may have been ratified, but implementing the infrastructure of a unified Hills-Fremont nation is going to be quite an undertaking."

"Then it's a good thing you'll have one of Clarion's finest political minds at your side," Dad says.

"Seriously, Mom?" I ask her. "You want me to help? Like a real ambassador?"

"It's going to be a tricky time, Lana. We're going to need all the help we can get."

I can't believe how much things have changed. A few weeks ago, I was dreading spending even a minute with my mom. But now I can't wait to learn from her. She knew *exactly* how to handle the Finnian situation when I felt so stuck. She's exactly the kind of ruler I want to be: one who doesn't hesitate to take charge, even during the difficult moments.

"And maybe . . . maybe we could organize a diplomatic mission to Quimby?" I ask. Making things right with Quimby—both the person and the duchy—is way up there on my list of priorities on land (a list that also includes doing more research on half-human, half-mer mind reading, because seriously, we have a lot more to learn). Hopefully, Quimby will give me another chance.

"Sure." Mom smiles. "We could always use more corn."

"It's going to be a long month, but I know you're in good hands." Dad sighs. "I'll miss you, Cuttlefish."

"I'll miss you, too, Dad." There's an uncomfortable lump in my throat. I *will* miss him, but I know this is the right thing for me. "See you soon, Aarav." I turn to my little brother and give him a huge hug.

"It won't be the same without you at home," he says into my hair. "But we'll survive. I'm just glad I never developed this mind-reading thing," he jokes.

"Me too." I laugh. "You couldn't handle it."

"Just like you can't handle losing at Catch the Crab."

"Hey!" I protest. "What are you talking about? I am *gracious* in defeat! You probably just can't remember because I'm so good, I almost never lose!"

It's not Aarav's fault that he's got the athletic ability of a sea cucumber.

"Keep telling yourself that, blobfish!" Aarav does a funny little dance as he boogies down the dock, then jumps off into the water. I laugh, watching him disappear below the waves. Moments later, his head pops up with a splash right at Dad's side. They hug, then wave at me, and I'm waving back, smiling so big my cheeks hurt.

With one final wave, Dad and Aarav disappear into the sea, followed by the rest of the royal retinue. It's an unbelievably calm day, the ocean almost smooth as glass. I shade my eyes with my hand as I look out over the horizon, the water seemingly limitless before me.

"Come on, Lana," Mom says gently, nudging me with her shoulder. She holds out her hand, and I take it. "Let's go home."

And even though I'm walking away from the water, that's exactly where I'm going.

ACKNOWLEDGMENTS

I grew up just a few blocks from Long Island Sound, and I spent every summer of my childhood pretending to be a mermaid, collecting shells, talking to seagulls, avoiding jellyfish, and swimming out farther than my mom would have liked. I feel so lucky that I got to tell Lana's story and make some of my little-kid dreams come true.

Molly Ker Hawn, my poetic noble land-mermaid of an agent: You make everything possible. Thank you.

To my two incredible editors: Thank you to Kieran Scott for entrusting me with Lana's story and helping me create her, and thank you to Rachel Stark for helping me find Lana's tail-kicking political prowess. Thanks to you two, this princess definitely makes waves.

Thank you to Molly Horton Booth and Crystal Cestari for reading a draft exactly when I needed it most. The fact that you both pretended all my fish puns were good really speaks to what kind and wonderful friends you are.

Max, you may be old hat, but you're my old hat. The best old hat, really.

Ezra, you helped not at all; in fact, you hindered, but I love you so much.

Dad, I'm sorry about all the times I tried to badger you into going swimming when you didn't have the correct glasses situation.

Alison, remember when I tried to convince you that the swimming teacher at the Y was a merman? He was not.

Mom, thank you for always being the first one in the water with me, for drawing mermaids, telling mermaid stories, reading mermaid books, watching mermaid movies, and making mermaid costumes. You're the real mermaid in our family.